*"A*__ ___ ___ ___ ___
feeding a thief and a liar?"

Camille's question was laced with a challenge.

Baylor turned quickly to face her. "What would you say if I told you I believe your story?"

"I'd say *you're* the liar. But don't worry, I'm not going to run away again," she said. "I changed my mind. I thought about this whole thing while I took a bath, and I decided that if I've been accused of stealing something, I ought to stick around long enough to clear myself."

"And how do you propose to do that?" Baylor asked.

"I figure we'd be a lot more successful if we combined our resources."

"We? You mean, you and me, together? Your brains and my brawn?"

"My logic and your street smarts," she corrected him gently. "So what do you say?"

He didn't have to think long. "You're on, Smart Stuff. You got yourself a partner." The idea appealed to him for more reasons than one....

Dear Reader,

Happy holidays! Though it may be cold outside, it's always warmed by the festivities of this special season. Everyone at Silhouette Books wishes you joy and cheer at this wonderful time of the year.

In December, we have some heartwarming books to take the chill off the weather. The final title in our DIAMOND JUBILEE celebration is *Only the Nanny Knows for Sure* by Phyllis Halldorson. Don't miss this tender love story about a nanny who has a secret . . . and a handsome hero who doesn't stand a ghost of a chance at remaining a bachelor!

The DIAMOND JUBILEE—Silhouette Romance's tenth anniversary celebration—is our way of saying thanks to you, our readers. To symbolize the timelessness of love, as well as the modern gift of the tenth anniversary, we've presented readers with a DIAMOND JUBILEE Silhouette Romance each month in 1990, penned by one of your favorite Silhouette Romance authors. It's been a wonderful year of love and romance here at Silhouette Books, and we hope that you've enjoyed our DIAMOND JUBILEE celebration. Saying thanks has never been so much fun!

And that's not all! There are six books a month from Silhouette Romance—stories by wonderful writers who time and time again bring home the magic of love. And we've got a lot of exciting events planned for 1991. In January, look for Marie Ferrarella's *The Undoing of Justin Starbuck*—the first book in the WRITTEN IN THE STARS series. Each month in 1991, we're proud to present readers with a book that focuses on the hero—and his Zodiac sign. Be sure to watch for that mysterious Capricorn man . . . and then meet Mr. Aquarius in *Man from the North Country* by Laurie Paige in February.

1991 is sure to be extra special. With works by authors such as Diana Palmer (don't miss her upcoming Long, Tall Texan!), Annette Broadrick, Nora Roberts and so many other talented writers, how could it not be? It's always celebration time at Silhouette Romance—the celebration of love.

I hope you'll enjoy this book and all of the stories to come. Come home to romance—Silhouette Romance—for always!

Sincerely,

Tara Gavin
Senior Editor

KAREN LEABO

Smart
Stuff

Silhouette *Romance*

Published by Silhouette Books New York

America's Publisher of Contemporary Romance

SILHOUETTE BOOKS
300 E. 42nd St., New York, N.Y. 10017

ISBN: 0-373-08764-0

First Silhouette Books printing December 1990

Printed in the U.S.A.

Books by Karen Leabo

Silhouette Romance

Roses Have Thorns #648
Ten Days in Paradise #692
Domestic Bliss #707
Full Bloom #731
Smart Stuff #764

KAREN LEABO

credits her fourth-grade teacher with initially spark-
ing her interest in creative writing. She was determined at an early age to have her work published.
When she was in the eighth grade, she wrote a children's book and convinced her school yearbook publisher to put it in print.

Karen was born and raised in Dallas but now lives in
Kansas City, Missouri. She has worked as a magazine
art director, a free-lance writer and a textbook editor,
but now she keeps herself busy full-time writing about
romance.

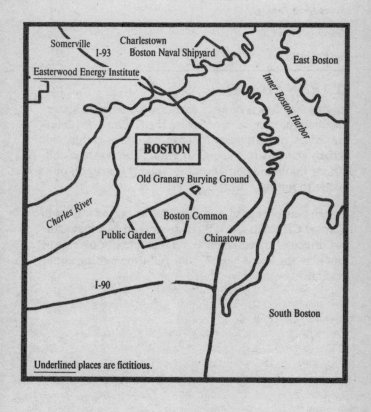

Somerville
I-93
Charlestown
Boston Naval Shipyard
East Boston

Easterwood Energy Institute

Inner Boston Harbor

BOSTON

Old Granary Burying Ground

Charles River

Boston Common

Public Garden

Chinatown

I-90

South Boston

Underlined places are fictitious.

Prologue

The plum trees along Energy Drive were a riot of color, their soft pink blooms exploding in the bright April sun. For the first time in her adult life, Camille Gordon saw spring. The awesome beauty of it stole her breath away, and she found herself pausing to close her eyes and inhale the heady fragrance of burgeoning life.

Was spring always this spectacular? she wondered. Or had she simply not noticed? She was noticing now, by God. She wouldn't let such things escape her attention ever again.

With renewed purpose she readjusted the straps of her backpack and resumed her stride, increasing the distance between herself and Easterwood Energy Institute—her self-imposed prison for the past three years. She spared one look over her shoulder, but no one seemed to notice her departure. Why would they? There was nothing remarkable about her appearance. She looked just like the hundreds of other young, casually dressed employees who knocked off work at five o'clock and headed for the bus stop at the end of the street.

She received her first test in modern living when the bus arrived. She had no idea whether the single token she clutched in her sweaty palm would be sufficient to gain her transportation anywhere. Maybe it took two or three. She watched the man in front of her as he deposited one token into a contraption just inside the door. Then she did the same, holding her breath, waiting to be pointed out as an imposter. But again no one took notice of her.

When the bus was ten minutes away from Easterwood, Camille breathed a true sigh of relief. She'd done it. She'd left her old job and her old life behind. She had fifty dollars in her pocket; she had an account bearing her name at the Pilgrim's Bank of Boston, the balance of which she'd discover tomorrow; and she had a box of computer diskettes in her backpack that she hoped would add up to a new future.

Chapter One

Baylor Pierce absently rubbed the two-day stubble on his chin as he tried to think of a nice way to say no to Paul. It wasn't going to be easy. Paul Kincaid had been his closest friend for more than fifteen years.

Two months ago, Baylor would have performed this favor for Paul without a second thought. But things were different now. Baylor had taken a leave of absence from the Boston Police Department precisely to avoid this kind of work. The last thing he needed was to go chasing after some bubble-headed employee who'd run away from her job.

"Camille has no friends or family in Boston, no place to stay," Paul said from behind the broad expanse of his glossy walnut desk. "You've got to find her before she gets into trouble."

The word "no" was on the tip of Baylor's tongue when Paul shoved a manila file across the desk and flipped it open. A young woman in a photo stared back at him with enormous hazel eyes and a wistful expression that brought a tightness to the back of Baylor's throat.

"Why do you want her back so badly?" Baylor asked, perusing the essentials of the personnel file. *Mary Camille Gordon.* DOB put her at age twenty-five. Tenure at Easterwood Energy Institute, three years. "What's so special about her?"

"I have personal reasons for wanting her back."

Baylor's head jerked up, and he fixed his friend with a stare that could have melted a polar ice cap. Paul was being deliberately evasive, and that wasn't like him. "Are you involved with this girl?" Baylor asked.

Paul almost smiled. "Not in the way you mean. But I am fond of her. I've known Camille since she was a kid— her father used to be head of Easterwood's Nuclear Physics department, so she practically grew up here. I can't imagine anything that would make her leave in such haste, and frankly I'm worried."

Baylor leaned back, pretending disinterest in the file. "If she works for you, she's an above-average-intelligent woman. She obviously became fed up with slaving away in that tomb of a laboratory you're so crazy about—really, Paul, a window or two wouldn't hurt. Maybe it was just time for her to move on."

But Paul was shaking his head. "It's not that simple. In the first place..." He hesitated while he lit a cigarette. "In the first place, she's not just above-average intelligent. Take another look at that file."

Baylor did, noting first the year she graduated from high school. He did some quick math. "High school diploma at age sixteen?"

"By examination. Her parents got some kind of special permission to educate her at home, which they apparently did very well. Keep reading."

The more Baylor read, the more astonished he became. Camille Gordon had advanced through MIT undergraduate—with a double major—in three years, had two master's degrees after another eighteen months, and had attained her doctorate in nuclear physics by the time she was twenty-two. "What kind of IQ does she have, for God's sake?" he asked.

Paul leaned forward on his elbows. "High enough. That's the problem. She can dismantle my computer and put it back together again in under thirty minutes. But she's so absentminded, she can hardly remember to tie her shoes. Camille Gordon doesn't have the survival instinct God gave a housefly."

That fact didn't surprise Baylor. "Dad is that way," he said absently as long-ago memories suddenly came into sharp focus. "You remember, don't you? Sometimes, when he became engrossed in his research, my mother had to remind him to eat and sleep and change his socks."

"Exactly," Paul agreed. "But unlike your father, Camille has never had to fend for herself. Her parents were . . . idiosyncratic, shall we say? They recognized their daughter's genius very early on, and they took it upon themselves to nurture her intelligence to the nth degree. They decided which school she'd attend, what degrees she would seek, and ultimately what career path she would take. They controlled every aspect of her life. And when they died—both of them within a year, unfortunately—I sort of inherited her. Ever since she came to work here, Easterwood has provided all of her basic needs—housing, food, clothes, medical care."

"My God, Paul, what kind of company is this? Sounds more like a prison than—"

"She wanted it that way. She had no idea how to handle money or prepare meals, and she didn't want to learn.

All she wanted was to devote a hundred percent of her energy to her work. Her paychecks are deposited directly into a savings account—I doubt she even knows where the account is kept or how much money she has. The last time she went out into the real world was last Christmas, when she was determined to do some shopping, and even then she didn't want to go by herself.''

"I went with her," said a deep female voice from behind Baylor. He swiveled around to see Nita Carter, Paul's silver-haired secretary, swishing toward them with her usual efficiency, holding a tray with two delicate china cups, sugar, cream, and spoons for stirring. She set the tray down on the corner of Paul's desk.

"Thank you, Nita," Paul said. "You remember Baylor Pierce, don't you?"

"Yes, of course. How are you, Mr. Pierce?"

Automatically Baylor stood as Nita nodded and gave a tight little smile. He started to offer his hand, then thought better of it. From what he remembered, Nita wasn't the type of woman who shook hands. She was the old-fashioned sort of secretary who was fiercely protective of Paul, following him around like a mother hen to remind him of appointments and bring him coffee. Despite her high-tech environment, she was intimidated by computers and insisted on hanging on to her old electric typewriter.

Baylor wasn't surprised to see her still working at eight o'clock in the evening, either. No one who worked for Paul got away with a forty-hour week.

"Camille was so intimidated by the outside world, Mr. Pierce," Nita said, nervously fingering the rhinestone chain that fastened the sweater draped over her shoulders. "The Christmas shopping really unnerved her. We had to come back here almost immediately. And she certainly never went anywhere alone. I just don't understand why she would leave without telling *me*—'' Her voice cracked, and she blinked her eyes rapidly. ''I'm sorry. I'll bring the coffeepot in.''

''Nita was devoted to Camille,'' Paul explained after the secretary had departed. ''She never had children of her own, and when Camille arrived, Nita just took her under her wing. She's as baffled and hurt by Camille's disappearance as I am.''

''So let me get this straight,'' Baylor said. ''Camille Gordon was last seen about three o'clock today, leaving the dentist's office. And when you tried to find her later, you discovered she'd signed out at around five o'clock.''

Paul nodded. ''And it doesn't sound like she's coming back. She left me a voice mail message.''

''Do you still have the recording?'' Baylor asked. ''I want to hear it.''

Paul shrugged as he picked up the phone and punched in a code. Then he handed the receiver to Baylor.

''There's no way to explain this, Paul,'' said a soft, husky voice into Baylor's ear, ''but I have to leave Easterwood. Please try to understand. I'm sorry about M23—'' The message ended with a strange abruptness.

The voice left Baylor with a peculiar ache in the pit of his stomach. ''What the hell is M23?'' he asked.

''It's a project Camille and I were working on. I can't tell you what it is, exactly, but it's enough for you to know that M23 could change the way the world thinks about energy. It's still years away from completion, but a lot of people out there would like to get their hands on it.''

''Are you afraid Camille will sell it?''

''No!'' Paul said emphatically. ''No, I trust her. But she was excited about the project, and her natural inclination might be to talk about it—to the wrong person. She would be an easy mark for an unscrupulous competitor, of which

Easterwood has plenty. So you see why I'm in such a hurry to get her back.''

Aha. Here was the heart of the matter, Baylor thought. Paul might be concerned about Camille, but what he really wanted was to protect his corporate secrets.

"Paul, I can't bring her back if she doesn't want to come.''

''But you'll try?''

Baylor gave a loud sigh of resignation. He felt his resolve slipping. When he spared one more glance at the hazel eyes in Camille's photograph, his decision was made. ''All right, I'll try to find her—strictly unofficial, you understand.''

Paul looked relieved.

Once Baylor was committed to pursuing Camille, he pored over her personnel file, memorizing her description and every relevant detail that might point to her destination. She had no living relatives to which she might flee, and Paul insisted that she had no close friends among the company employees other than Nita and himself.

With no one to help her, where could she have gone?

Baylor had a partial answer to that question a few minutes later, as he and Paul took a tour of the one-bedroom apartment Camille had occupied at Easterwood. It was a utilitarian place, devoid of color or style. There were no pictures on the walls, no knickknacks on the shelves. The few items of clothing in her closet were unstructured, functional, with not a designer label in the bunch. Her sheets were white.

But the apartment did yield one important clue. A blank notepad sat on her desk next to her personal computer. By applying a lead pencil lightly to the surface of the pad, the last thing she'd written appeared—a long number and an address.

Baylor held it out to Paul. "Recognize this?"

Paul studied it for a moment, then frowned. "The address belongs to the Pilgrim's Bank downtown."

"The other must be her account number," said Baylor. "Survival instincts of a housefly, huh? Looks like her bolt for freedom was premeditated." Then a smile slowly spread across his face.

"What? What are you thinking?"

"She left here after the banks were closed. She can't get far without money. My guess is she'll head for Pilgrim's first thing tomorrow morning. I'll be there, waiting for her."

Camille sat in a comfortably upholstered chair in the corner of the bank lobby, trying not to fidget as she waited for a Mr. Flammond to return. She'd had no idea how complicated a simple financial transaction could be.

Why couldn't she just order some checks, then withdraw enough cash to tide her over for a few days until the checks arrived? But no, her request had been too complex for the bank teller to handle. She'd been referred to this Mr. Flammond, the new accounts clerk, who had eyed her with a great deal of suspicion before disappearing to retrieve some forms he needed to open a checking account for her.

It wasn't just the bank that proved perplexing. So were buses and subways with their funny tokens and indecipherable route maps, and taxis, which should have charged by the mile but which, quite illogically, also charged according to the time it took to get from point A to point B. Camille had questioned one driver about this, objecting that the passenger shouldn't be penalized if the driver didn't have enough sense to get out of rush-hour traffic.

He'd laughed at her inquisitiveness and then drove off with her change, instead of waiting for her to tip him.

And speaking of tips! If a helpful doorman hadn't given her a five-minute lesson on how much to leave here and there to various people, she might still be wandering around Boston stiffing waitresses and bellhops. That thought left her wondering, as she gazed at her marble-and-glass surroundings—was she supposed to tip at a bank?

Her musings halted abruptly when she saw the man in the gray raincoat looking at her. He wasn't staring, exactly, but when their eyes met, he averted his gaze too hastily.

Since he was now so obviously engrossed in his own business, a stack of papers that he shuffled through importantly while standing in line at a teller window, she took the opportunity to study him. The way he slouched in his nondescript clothes, he wouldn't normally have captured her attention. But now that she'd noticed him, she could see he had a more-than-handsome face. His dark hair, though fairly short, still managed to curl over his high forehead. He had sharp, prominent cheekbones, a thin, determined mouth, a square jaw. His classic features were marred only by his slightly crooked nose.

Camille smiled unconsciously. The nose was the only thing that prevented him from being too pretty.

"Miss Gordon?"

Her attention was drawn back to Mr. Flammond, who had returned to his desk with some official-looking papers. "Yes?"

"If you'll just fill these out, we'll order your personalized checks. And here's a book of temporary checks to tide you over."

"Oh." Camille started to fill out the forms, but she paused when she came to the blanks for her address. "Mr. Flammond, I have a problem. I don't have an address yet. I haven't found a place to live."

His forehead creased. "You have to have an address, or at least a Post Office box, before you can open a checking account," he said primly. "I suggest you withdraw some cash from your savings account, buy some traveler's checks to be on the safe side, then come back when you have an address." He sniffed and studied his fingernails, as if that were the end of it.

Exasperated, she left Mr. Flammond's desk in a huff and stalked over to the line of people waiting in front of the teller windows, where a sign advertised that traveler's checks were sold. The man in the gray raincoat was gone. She felt a vague sense of disappointment and wondered what it meant.

"I just located her," Baylor said into the receiver of the pay phone, within sight of the bank's revolving front door.

"For God's sake, don't lose her," Paul said urgently, his voice rife with tension. "But don't tip her off that you've found her. There's been a new development."

"What?" Baylor barked as his quarry exited the bank and walked in the opposite direction.

"When I went to work this morning, I discovered that Project M23 is gone. Every single byte of data disappeared from the computer, right along with Camille. She must have circumvented the antitheft measures. Even the backup diskettes have been erased and the data replaced with some nonsense."

"Oh, hell." Baylor had known he'd regret getting involved. Chasing down a runaway employee was distasteful enough; chasing down a world-class thief was something else again.

"Wait a minute," Baylor said. "I thought you trusted Camille."

"I do...I mean, I did. But the facts speak for themselves. I don't want to believe she stole the project, but I don't have much choice, do I?"

"Call the police," Baylor said decisively. "Go through normal channels. I'll keep an eye on her until—"

"I can't go through normal police channels," Paul said urgently. "The publicity would jeopardize the whole project, and it might put Camille in danger. I don't want her hurt. She was a friend, Baylor. I can't believe she'd betray me like this unless something was terribly wrong. You're the only one I trust to find out what's going on."

He watched as Camille turned the corner; he was losing her. "Gotta go," Baylor said. "I'll check back with you when I get a chance."

He hung up and started down the street at a sprint, cursing himself in three different languages—first for getting roped into this mess, and second for being such a sloppy tail. Camille had spotted him inside the bank. He'd have to be more careful.

When he peered around the corner, he saw her paused in front of a newsstand. Thank God he hadn't lost her. On one level he wished he'd never heard of Camille Gordon. But he couldn't deny that the adrenaline pumping through his veins, brought on by the prospect of a chase, felt good. Something appealed to him about matching wits with a genius. If he could outmaneuver her, it would prove—

It would prove nothing, dammit.

Now that the sky had cleared, it was tolerably warm in the sunshine. Baylor watched as she bought a newspaper and settled onto a bench to read. He found a table at a deserted outdoor café where he could keep watch.

It occurred to him, as he nursed a paper cup full of coffee, that he didn't like thinking of Camille as a thief. Though logic and ten years on the police force had taught him that there was no such thing as a criminal "type," this woman didn't look as if she could pilfer a pack of gum, much less a multimillion-dollar project.

His first glimpse of her in the bank this morning had made him feel compassion, not suspicion. He couldn't have missed her; among the throng of bustling businesspersons, she had reminded him of a lost child, her petite five-foot-three frame dwarfed even further by the imposing proportions of the bank.

She had looked just as she had in her photo, with long, light brown hair pulled back from her face in a braid, her huge hazel eyes contemplating her surroundings with a trace of wonder. She'd still worn the clothes in which she'd last been seen, a tan corduroy skirt with a white blouse, an oversized brown cardigan, and a navy pea jacket. An army green backpack was slung carelessly over one shoulder. The effect was hardly flattering. Yet there was something about her that stirred his imagination. Maybe it was the determination he saw in the set of her full mouth, or the way she'd calmly surveyed the lobby, then resolutely stepped in line at a teller window.

No matter what Paul thought, Camille was a survivor. She might lack practical experience, but she seemed to be attacking her problems logically. Baylor had to respect anyone who could survive on sheer logic. He himself tended to rely on the vagaries of hunches and instinct. That's how he'd squeaked his way up the police department ladder.

His instincts told him Camille wasn't a criminal. Unfortunately something as intangible as instinct wasn't always reliable. He'd found that out the hard way.

There he was again! Camille peered around a clothing rack at the tall man from the bank, who was perusing a glass case of jewelry. He'd discarded his raincoat, but she couldn't mistake that face anywhere.

She thought she'd caught a glimpse of him over the top of her newspaper as she'd scanned the want ads, but then she'd chided herself for being fanciful. She should have trusted her own eyes. Was he following her?

"How did that work for you?" said a woman's voice from behind.

Startled, Camille whirled around to face the salesclerk who'd been helping her. Then she smiled and looked down at the garment she'd tried on, a sleeveless cotton shirtdress in a wild jungle print of blue, plum, and orange. The waist was cinched by a braided leather belt, and the full skirt billowed down to midcalf. "It's perfect," she said. "I'll take it." On impulse she also bought a wide-brimmed blue straw hat and a pair of sunglasses, mentally adding up the purchases in her head and computing sales tax. She had the exact change in her hand by the time the salesclerk gave her the total.

When next she checked the jewelry counter, the man was gone. But she had an eerie feeling she hadn't seen the last of him.

She left the department store and continued toward her original destination, an apartment locater service. She'd been trying to get there all morning, but she kept getting distracted by colorful displays of spring clothes and accessories. With a thick wad of traveler's checks in her backpack, she could afford to buy some clothes and still have plenty left over for a deposit on an apartment. So she'd wandered through store after store, adding to her purchases.

Now, loaded down by two huge shopping bags filled with bright, breezy dresses, flashy cotton sweaters, scarves, fashionable jeans, some bangle bracelets, and two pairs of shoes, she was determined to find an apartment—one with big closets. She'd never realized how much fun shopping could be.

The hairs on the back of her neck stood at attention as she entered a high-rise office building, and she knew the man was still following her. Oddly enough, that knowledge didn't particularly bother her. If the guy meant her harm, he'd have made his move by now. No, he was merely watching. Paul had no doubt hired someone to find her and make sure she was all right. He was probably worried sick.

Maybe she'd telephone Paul later and reassure him. But no; if she made contact with him, he'd find a way to talk her into coming back. Camille was all too susceptible to his persuasive arguments.

Choosing an apartment turned out to be the most difficult task she'd faced to date. The woman at the locater service bombarded her with questions. How many bedrooms do you want? How many baths? What area of the city is best? Do you want a garage? Swimming pool?

Camille finally became fed up. "I need a place now, today," she said. "I don't care where, as long as it's safe, comfortable, and within a reasonable distance of a bus or subway. Just pick out some place and tell me how much I'll have to pay."

"Well, now, dear, that sounds fine but there's still the matter of the rental application—"

"I'll pay a year's rent in advance."

The woman's manner changed swiftly. "Ah, I see. Come back in two hours and I'll have everything ready."

Money does talk, Camille mused as she exited the building. What could she do to kill two hours? She saw a posh-looking beauty salon across the street, and her decision was made.

A few minutes later, as she leaned back in the reclining chair with warm water sluicing through her long hair, she sighed with genuine delight. Now she understood the meaning of the word "pampered," and it was heaven! The stylist's fingers firmly massaged Camille's scalp as the floral scent of the shampoo drifted around her.

She had planned on simply having her hair trimmed and styled, but somehow she got talked into a facial and a sorely needed lesson in cosmetics. Where had she acquired this consuming need to be feminine and frivolous? she wondered. But even as the question occurred to her, she knew the blame lay with that blasted magazine in the dentist's office.

Of course, picking up that fashion magazine was only one link in a series of random events yesterday that had added up to a drastic change in Camille's life. First there was the rock video she'd glimpsed as she'd walked through the employee lounge on her way to Easterwood's dentist. Camille had stopped suddenly and stared at the image of the unidentified female singer on the screen, transfixed by the bright, outrageous clothes, the dramatic makeup and hair, the suggestive gyrations of her dance—all of it so wonderfully exotic and enviable. Camille had felt a peculiar sensation in the pit of her stomach, an almost physical pain that made her wonder if she wasn't coming down with something.

She'd hurried on to the dentist's office, shaking off the unfamiliar feelings. But Dr. Fisher was running behind schedule, forcing Camille to cool her heels in the waiting room. Because she'd forgotten to bring along one of her scientific journals to read, she absently picked up a glossy women's magazine. Again she'd been confronted with colorful, stylish clothing and chic hairstyles, not to mention a host of persuasive advertisements for cosmetics and perfume, plus articles on food, cinema, travel, love and sex. Suddenly it hit her that a huge world existed outside her microcosm of textbooks and computers, and she wanted to experience it. A wave of longing had washed over her, bringing her close to tears.

A few minutes later, as she'd reclined in the dentist's chair, mildly sedated while Dr. Fisher repaired a cracked filling, all sorts of crazy thoughts had roiled inside her head—thoughts of freedom and a life-style she might have out in the real world.

Her fantasies might have remained just that if she hadn't found the bus token. It had lain in the hallway outside the dentist's office, looking for all the world as if fate had dropped it there just for Camille. Furtively she'd scooped it off the floor and deposited it into the pocket of her cardigan. Her decision to leave Easterwood had been made. Just like that.

Camille emerged from the salon looking and feeling like a different woman. She'd exchanged her blah clothing for one of her sizzling new dresses. Her hair was now a mass of chestnut curls dancing about her face and trailing down her back. Her makeup looked cover-girl perfect. She appeared so different, in fact, that she strolled within inches of the man who'd been following her all day and he never recognized her.

That gave her a great idea.

"I lost her," Baylor said into another pay phone as he gazed out over the Boston Common. The grass was just starting to show bits of green. "She walked into a beauty salon and never came out again. I think she was on to me, Paul. She must have slipped out a back door."

"I'm ruined," Paul groaned.

"Don't be so melodramatic. She's been working with an apartment locating service. If I pull my standard police detective speech, they'll give me the address of the apartment she rented."

"And meanwhile she might have sold M23 a dozen times over."

"I don't think so, Paul. She doesn't act like a woman who's in the process of committing a multimillion-dollar theft."

"Then what does she act like?" Paul demanded.

"Like a woman who's been released from prison. Your naive little genius has been systematically wiping out the inventory of every store on Boylston Street."

"Camille? Shopping? Are you sure you've been following the right girl?"

"Yup. You seriously underestimated her survival instinct, my friend. I'll get back to you when I have something."

Baylor hung up, turned, and ran smack into a brightly dressed woman. Startled, he took a half step backward, then reached out to steady her. "Sorry," he murmured automatically, just as his mind registered recognition. It was *her*. He barely managed to hide his shock.

"Are you okay?" he asked when she didn't continue on her path up the sidewalk.

"Fine." She stared up at him with a self-satisfied smirk. "You don't recognize me, do you?"

"Am I supposed to?" he shot back, careful to avoid lying outright.

"I thought you might, since you've been following me all day."

He sighed inwardly. So much for outmaneuvering the genius. He gave her his most winsome smile while he tried to think of a plausible reason for his interest in her. "I didn't think you'd notice me. I'm sorry, really. I didn't mean to frighten you."

"What *did* you mean to do?" she asked.

"It's...it's not important," he answered. An elderly woman had approached them and obviously wanted to use the phone, so Baylor shoved his hands in his pockets and started walking up the street.

Camille followed. "Yes it is important," she insisted. "Paul sent you to spy on me, didn't he? That's who you were talking to on the phone."

Spy? That was an interesting choice of words. "Paul who?" Baylor asked, wondering how much of his phone conversation she'd overheard.

"You know darn well who he is. And you can report back to him that I'm just fine. By the end of the day I'll have a place to live, I've got plenty of money, and I have a new career in mind."

A new career? Selling secrets, perhaps? "Look," Baylor said, "never mind about this Paul. I followed you because..." *Why?* "Because I'm attracted to you." *Oh, hell.* What had made him say that?

Camille stopped walking. "To me? You were attracted to *me*?"

"Is that so surprising?"

"Yes. I'm not exactly the kind of woman men follow through the streets."

"Obviously you are." His frank appraisal caused her to blush. Baylor noticed then that she had an appealing dusting of freckles across her nose.

They walked in silence for a minute or two. "Suppose I said I was attracted to you, too," she suggested cautiously. "What happens next?"

"Whoa, wait a minute. What about this Paul?" Baylor asked, to give his ignorance act a little more credence. "He's not your husband, is he?"

Camille laughed in a husky, unconsciously sexy way. Baylor was so entranced and distracted by it he almost tripped on his own feet. "Paul's my employer—former employer, that is. As of yesterday I'm completely unencumbered—no job, no husband, no possessions except the ones on my—oh, no!"

"What's wrong?" he asked as she stopped in the middle of the sidewalk, a horrified expression on her face.

"My backpack! I must have left it somewhere. I have to get it back. There's something irreplaceable in it, not to mention all my traveler's checks."

She looked and sounded so distraught, Baylor had to fight the urge to put an arm around her delicate shoulders and comfort her. But no wonder she was upset. The "something irreplaceable" had to be connected with M23. If he didn't help her find her backpack, everyone would lose.

"All right, calm down," he said soothingly. "Where did you last have it?"

She closed her eyes. "Let me think a minute...yes, I had it at the beauty salon because I remember taking my traveler's checks out to pay for everything. I changed my clothes, and then—"

"I like the new dress," Baylor couldn't help saying.

"Shh! Don't distract me. I came out of the beauty shop and passed right by you." She opened her eyes and looked at him. "You don't remember seeing me, do you?"

He shook his head, wondering how he could have missed her.

"That's when I started following you."

"*You* followed *me*?" He really was slipping, if a woman in a neon dress and a blue hat could follow him for more than an hour and escape his notice.

"I wanted to see where you'd go. I thought you'd meet with Paul, or call him—are you sure that wasn't him on the phone?"

"Forget the phone call," he said impatiently. "Now, about the backpack?" He tried to sound eager to help rather than frantic.

"Oh, yes." She closed her eyes again. "You wandered into that little drugstore, remember? I followed, and I—oh, I know. I bought a granola bar, so I had to have the backpack then. Yes. Yes! I left it sitting on the floor by the cash register. That's it!" She'd already started off at a brisk walk in the direction of the drugstore.

Baylor stepped in beside her, resisting the urge to break into a run. It would be a miracle if the backpack was still there.

The young man behind the cash register at the drugstore confirmed Baylor's worst fears. When Camille asked about the backpack, he stared at her myopically for several moments, looking utterly confused.

"Yes, there *was* a backpack," he finally said. "I stuck it behind the counter, but a kid came in a few minutes ago and claimed it. He described it in detail, and since I didn't see who left it behind..." He shrugged.

"But it was mine," Camille objected.

"How was I to know? The kid probably saw you walk away from it. And when you didn't come back right away...I think you've been ripped off, lady."

Camille looked as if someone had kicked her in the stomach.

Chapter Two

Baylor tried to be analytical about Camille's distress. It only pointed to her guilt, didn't it? Why would she be so distraught otherwise? But again, he had to force himself not to go to her, comfort her. His first priority was to retrieve Project M23 for Paul.

Damn! He'd never known a thief with such big hazel eyes and adorable freckles.

"Can you describe the kid?" he asked the cashier, falling back on standard police procedure. Find out as much as possible about the perp. Maybe there was still hope.

"He was Asian," the young cashier answered, scrunching up his face as he tried to remember, "probably about fifteen or sixteen. Just a street kid—you know the kind. Blue jeans, T-shirt—and a fatigue jacket with the sleeves cut out."

"Did you happen to notice which way he went?" Baylor asked.

"Uh, up the street toward . . . no, maybe the other way. Gee, I can't really remember. Do you want I should call the police?"

"No," both Baylor and Camille answered simultaneously.

"It's not that important," Camille said in a soft voice. "I can get the traveler's checks replaced. The rest of the stuff . . ." She shrugged. "It wasn't valuable, not to anyone except me."

Mechanically Baylor thanked the cashier, though for what he wasn't sure.

"Did you lose something of sentimental value?" Baylor asked with almost-genuine concern as they exited the drugstore. No matter what the facts dictated, he was having a hard time thinking of Camille as someone who'd just lost a parcel of stolen scientific data. He had to fight an irrational urge to *help* her.

"It was something very personal, that's all." She paused at the corner. "Look, Mr. . . . I don't even know your name."

"Baylor Pierce."

"Mr. Pierce—"

"Baylor," he corrected her.

"Baylor, I appreciate your concern, but I have to get back to the bank if I want to do anything about my traveler's checks today. So I'll say goodbye now." She held out her hand.

He ignored it and looked at his watch. "It's five minutes till five. I'm sure the bank is already closed."

"Oh, no." She let out a long, hopeless-sounding sigh. "I had no idea it was so late. Now what am I going to do?"

Didn't she know about the toll-free number she could call twenty-four hours a day to get the checks replaced? Apparently not. He couldn't see his way clear to tell her about it, either. He wanted her off-balance. "You could have dinner with me," he suggested.

What a ridiculous idea, Camille thought. How would eating dinner with him help her situation? On the other hand, if she didn't accept the invitation she might very well go hungry tonight. One granola bar wouldn't fill her stomach for long.

But she couldn't accept dinner from someone she didn't know, could she? Hadn't Paul's secretary, Nita, drilled it into her head to be wary of strangers? But for some reason this particular stranger didn't worry Camille. In fact, just the opposite was true. There was something about his vivid green eyes that told her she could trust him, that he really was concerned for her welfare.

"C'mon, Camille, say yes," Baylor cajoled, obviously sensing her indecision.

She wondered how he knew her name. She remembered asking for his but couldn't recall introducing herself. "I don't think—"

"I know this great little seafood place that overlooks the Common. They have a baked stuffed sole with lobster sauce that is the most—"

"All right!" she said, smiling despite herself. "How can I say no? I'm starving, homeless, and temporarily destitute."

"The least you could do is tell me you can't resist my charm," he said with mock injury.

She had no snappy comeback to that—sparkling repartee had never been one of her strengths. So she merely smiled again and allowed him to carry her shopping bags, the business of names forgotten. He *was* charming—so charming, in fact, that the stolen backpack didn't seem such a disaster anymore. True, the diskettes she'd lost could never be replaced. But that didn't mean she had to abandon her plans for the future. She could still *try* to write her book. She'd just have to rely more on her memory, rather than on the notes and observations she'd been recording on her computer for the past few years.

"My car's just around the corner. Why don't we stash the shopping bags in my trunk?" Baylor suggested.

"What?" Camille snapped back to the present, annoyed with herself for getting lost in thought, even briefly.

"I said, let's stow your things in my trunk. Then we can walk to the restaurant. It's not far."

She nodded and vowed silently to avoid the extended mental vacations she was prone to. At Easterwood no one seemed to notice if she stared at a wall for two or three hours, trying to refine some abstract concept in her mind. But in the real world such behavior wasn't acceptable. Nita had pointed that out to her once during lunch, when Camille had been staring sightlessly into her cottage cheese, wondering if she could compute the atomic weight of a grain of pepper.

When she glanced up at Baylor again, she felt a funny, happy fluttering in her stomach and a warmth that seeped into the nether regions of her body. Though she'd never experienced it before, instinctively she knew what it meant—physical attraction. What did he feel when he looked at her? she wondered.

Suddenly the significance of this mutual attraction, if it really existed, hit Camille as if she'd been struck by a two-by-four. Where did such a thing lead? Dinner, first, she supposed. But ultimately? For reasons she didn't understand, she had to know. Thus far Baylor Pierce had accepted her as a normal woman. It was vital that he continue doing so—which meant she had to keep her background a secret. The mere mention of the words "nuclear physicist" might send him screaming into the night.

When they entered the restaurant, a deceptively plain-looking place called Deke's, a heavenly aroma instantly had Camille's mouth watering. The hour was still early for dinner, and since Deke's wasn't the type of place to attract a happy-hour crowd, they pretty much had their choice of tables. Baylor selected one next to a plate glass window overlooking the Common, where they could people-watch as the sun set. The first truly warm day of spring had brought cabin-fever victims to the park in droves. In one area a small crowd had gathered to listen to an impromptu jazz trio performance; in another, a softball game was forming.

At the moment, however, Camille was more interested in the food than the sights. She'd been too excited and nervous to eat much all day, and now she was suddenly ravenous. She studied her menu silently as she nibbled on a breadstick speckled with caraway seeds. To her dismay, she couldn't make a decision. She felt just as she had at the apartment locater office—bombarded with choices, some of them mystifying. *Blackened redfish?*

"What would you recommend?" she finally asked.

"A cup of New England clam chowder is absolutely required for your first course," Baylor replied. Then he asked, "Do you like orange roughy?"

She started to say she'd never had it. In truth, she didn't even know what it was. But Baylor might think that was odd. "One of my favorites," she fibbed.

Deke's was obviously one of Baylor's customary hangouts, judging from the fact that he claimed to know something about virtually every one of the dozens of available dishes. He skillfully lead Camille through the menu, extolling the merits of his favorites.

Camille was overwhelmed. She'd eaten out in restaurants before, but it had never been so important to order something she'd enjoy. Since comparative analysis didn't bring her any closer to a decision, she finally closed her eyes then opened them quickly and ordered the first thing she focused on, which happened to be the orange roughy.

The chowder was heavenly, Camille decided a few minutes later as she delicately sipped from her spoon. It was virtually overflowing with cream and butter. She'd forgotten how good food could be. Nothing at the Easterwood cafeteria could compare with this.

Her companion was even more remarkable. She'd always considered herself on the shy side, but Baylor had a knack for putting her at ease. He told amusing anecdotes, involved her in the conversation without being too inquisitive, and seemed to know a great deal of fascinating trivia on every subject from wine to the Red Sox.

Red Sox. Baseball? She should know, and she didn't. Somehow she brazened it out. If he caught on to the fact that she didn't understand the difference between a foul and a strike, he kept it to himself.

By the time their waiter brought the main course, Camille was more relaxed than she had been in days. Her newfound freedom was vastly more complex than she'd ever dreamed—better in some ways, more frightening in others. But she was living, *living,* like a normal person. She was testing herself, but she found joy and excitement in that. If she succeeded, fantastic. She could take pride in the fact that she'd challenged herself and met that challenge. She had no one to please but herself, no one watching over her, expecting miracles.

She gazed out the window, noting a group of teenagers standing in a cluster, watching the ball game. One of them carried a backpack much like hers, which reminded her of her biggest blunder so far, and her enthusiasm was momentarily dampened. How could she have been so careless? Yet the only one criticizing her was herself. Baylor hadn't so much as mentioned the word "absentminded," though that was a label she'd lived with her whole life.

She studied the group of kids in the park. The boys wore look-alike jackets with writing on back, proclaiming that they belonged to something called the Dawgs. They laughed and punched each other's arms in a rough-hewn camaraderie that Camille suddenly envied. She'd missed that sort of friendship growing up.

She'd been isolated as a child—her own fault, really. Twice her mother had insisted she try attending regular school. But she'd been just as isolated there, not to mention miserable. She simply hadn't known how to make friends, and no one had volunteered to show her. In college she'd had much the same problem. Her world had been confined to attending classes, supplemented by a lot of home study with her father. Her mother had shuttled her back and forth to the campus, so there had been no opportunity to make friends on a bus or in a cafeteria. Even if her intensive study had allowed her the leisure time to pursue social endeavours, she was sure she wouldn't have had much success.

As she continued to gaze at the kid with the backpack, something began to click. The kid was Asian, wearing jeans, T-shirt, and sleeveless fatigue jacket. And that backpack, with its distinctive bright aqua shoelace closure, didn't merely *look* like hers....

Baylor stopped talking midsentence when he realized Camille had tuned him out. Was he boring her stiff? Perhaps she was on a mental plane so far above his that she couldn't relate to his mundane conversation. But on second thought, he went a little easier on himself. She must have a lot on her mind right now.

To ease her back into the present he touched her hand. She gave a little jerk, then turned surprised eyes toward him.

"You haven't eaten much—" he started to say, but she interrupted him.

"That's my backpack!" she announced excitedly, pointing out the window. Before he could even react, she was out of her chair and dashing toward the door.

"Camille, wait!" he called after her. When she ignored him, he cursed under his breath, threw some money on the table to cover the bill, took one last longing look at the half-eaten baked cod he was leaving behind, then sprinted after her as surprised diners looked on.

She had a considerable head start on him, but she was by no means a fast runner, especially with her high-heeled pumps. By the time she'd crossed the street to the Common, his long strides had almost caught hers—and would have, too, if he hadn't had to stop for a truck. By the time the monstrous vehicle had passed, leaving a cloud of foul exhaust in its wake, Camille was already approaching a tough-looking gang of teenagers. The Dawgs, Baylor realized with a stab of apprehension. Though Boston didn't suffer the rampant gang warfare some other big cities did, the Dawgs were well known to the Boston police. The kids who made up the gang were often involved in petty crimes of various descriptions, and a few of them had dabbled in more serious offenses. Some of Baylor's own neighbors had felt the sting of the gang's criminal activities.

The kids saw Camille coming and instinctively made a circle around her, assuming their tough act. That didn't seem to faze her; she was initiating a conversation with them as Baylor drew closer. But as soon as they noticed his approach, the one with the backpack yelled something and the kids dispersed like roaches surprised by a light. Undaunted, Camille took out after her stolen property.

When Baylor finally caught up with her, he had to grab her by the shoulders and physically restrain her to get her to stop the chase. "Are you crazy?" he asked her. "You'll get yourself killed!"

Her eyes were directed over his shoulder toward the retreating youth. "Let go!" she demanded. "I'm going after my backpack."

"You stay here," Baylor ordered. "I'll catch the kid." He questioned his own sanity as he chased after the fleeing teenager. He had no more business than Camille confronting these young toughs, not when he was alone and without his gun.

The kid was fast, Baylor was willing to give him that. But Baylor was tall, and his long-legged sprint soon began to eat up the distance between himself and his quarry. They ran through the Common, across Charles Street, and into the Public Garden. Baylor could see that the boy was beginning to tire, while he himself was just beginning to hit his stride. He was glad he'd kept up his workouts since his leave of absence.

When he was within shouting distance of the teenager, he forgot for the moment that he wasn't officially on the force any longer. "Stop! Police!" he called out, realizing belatedly it was a stupid thing to do. But the boy slowed, stopped behind a weeping willow tree, and turned to face his pursuer.

"What do you want, man?" he cried. "I haven't done nothin'."

"I don't want to argue with you," Baylor said cautiously, holding his arms out from his sides to show he had no weapon. "I just want the backpack—" He stopped when he saw the glint of a knife in the teenager's hand.

"What for?" the boy demanded, protectively clutching the pack. "It's mine, you hear? Don't you come any nearer."

"Take it easy," Baylor said calmly. "Tell you what, I'll buy it from you. And you can keep the bag. I only want the contents."

The boy's interest seemed to pick up. "You got money on you?"

"Not on me," Baylor answered quickly as he sensed movement in his peripheral vision. Several other gang members had materialized as if out of nowhere, with steel glinting in their hands. Oh, swell.

"Says he's a cop," the one with the backpack told the others.

"He don't look like a cop," said another Dawg, a tall kid with white-blond hair and dark, dangerous eyes. "I don't see no gun, no badge." He sauntered close to Baylor, bringing an open switchblade close to his face.

Baylor stood still as a stone. "Look, I don't have any quarrel with the Dawgs and I don't want to start one." He saw a flash of blue and neon orange behind a bush. *Camille.* Dammit, why hadn't the little fool stayed put? She was about as inconspicuous as a five-alarm fire.

"Looks like you already started a quarrel," said the blonde. "What call do you have, chasing an innocent boy through the park?"

"Hey, come on, man," said one of the others. "Let's get out of here 'fore someone gets cut. If this guy really is a cop, he's liable to sic his cop friends on us, and we don't need that."

The others, through murmurs and nods, seemed to agree. The knives disappeared, the gang melted away—all but the blonde, who continued to hover around Baylor, flashing his knife and smiling unpleasantly.

Baylor decided he wouldn't have much trouble disarming the kid. But it would be better if he could avoid antagonizing a Dawg member. Revenge was a strong motivator, and Baylor didn't need the added complication of looking over his shoulder for the next few weeks.

The standoff was about to end. Baylor could sense it in the growing boredom showing in the kid's eyes. In a moment he'd close the knife and disappear into the encroaching darkness. But before that could happen, a streak of neon shot out from behind the bush and whacked the kid on the head with a high-heeled pump.

"Ouch!" The boy whirled around to see what had hit him. Baylor had no choice but to take advantage of the opening. He grabbed the boy's wrist, and in a split second the knife was in Baylor's possession.

"Get out of here before she decides to hit you again," Baylor said, adding a low growl for emphasis.

Looking confused, the boy hesitated for only a moment before turning and loping off to nurse his injured pride, rubbing his head and no doubt hoping his friends hadn't witnessed the indignity.

"Are you okay?" Camille asked, still clutching the shoe in one hand and her blue hat in the other.

Baylor wanted to wring her neck. The only thing that prevented it was the grave, concerned expression in her eyes. "Still alive, no thanks to you," he said tersely as he closed the huge switchblade and turned away from her, walking back toward Charles Street.

"What do you mean, 'no thanks to me'?" she objected as she tried to put her shoe on and hop after him at the same time. "If I hadn't followed you—"

"Everything would have worked out just fine," Baylor interrupted. "He was about half a heartbeat away from giving up when you came flying out of the bushes like— like Wonder Woman. Now we've made an enemy."

"I didn't ask you to chase after my backpack, you know," Camille said. "Why'd you take out after that kid in the first place?"

Baylor actually laughed. "If I hadn't, you would have. The Dawgs would have turned you into mincemeat."

"I was handling things just fine till you came along and scared them," she said softly. "They were listening to me. I could have reasoned with them, offered a reward or something. Now it's gone, and I'll never get it back."

"Mincemeat," he repeated. "Anyway, you can't reason with the Dawgs."

An uneasy silence rested on them as they walked back toward the lot where his car was parked. Camille was mentally cursing herself. Her impulsive behavior had endangered them both and spoiled their dinner. Now she'd probably never know what could have evolved between herself and Baylor Pierce. He no doubt thought she was crazy, and would rid himself of her at the first opportunity.

Then again, he had risked life and limb on her behalf. He wouldn't have done that if he didn't harbor at least a few positive feelings about her...or would he? Why had he chased that kid so relentlessly? Why had he offered to buy the backpack? Just for her?

"Are you really a cop?" she asked, hoping to lighten the mood with a little idle chitchat. They'd been having such a wonderful evening before she'd ruined it. "You never have told me what you do for a living."

"I used to be," he answered tersely.

"What do you do now?"

"I'm, uh, what did you call it? Unencumbered. Drifting." This last he said with a grim expression, causing Camille to wonder what had happened to make him turn his back on law enforcement. But even with her limited knowledge of social graces, she didn't figure it would be polite to ask.

"Are you looking for any particular kind of work?" she asked instead.

He shrugged. "I'm trying to figure that out."

"Maybe I could help you," she said, immediately realizing how pushy she sounded. But this was her one slim chance to salvage the evening. "What I mean is, if you want to talk about it, I listen awfully well. We could...have a drink somewhere." Mentally she patted herself on the back. That had sounded suitably sophisticated, suggesting a drink.

Baylor considered her offer. During the past couple of months a lot of people had offered a sympathetic ear, everyone from his mother to the police psychiatrist to the bartender who worked in the pub below his apartment. Camille's ear was the first that had tempted him.

All things considered, however, he knew he had to decline. Since she'd lost the stolen data, he had no need to draw out his association with her. He had other business to take care of—wheels to set in motion—if he wanted to recover that backpack. Her continued presence would hamper his work.

The best thing would be to find out where she was staying and inform Paul. Then Paul could contact her if he chose to.

"Maybe I better just drop you off at your hotel," Baylor suggested.

"That's all right, I'll walk," she said coolly.

"Don't be silly. It's no trouble for me to drop you off."

"No, thanks," she replied firmly.

That's what he deserved for rebuffing her friendly overture, Baylor thought with a pang of remorse mixed with irritation. If she insisted on walking to her hotel, he'd have to follow her again to find out where it was. "Don't forget the shopping bags in my trunk," he reminded her.

A long, strained silence followed, making the walk back to Baylor's car seem interminable. He had a nagging feeling that he'd really botched something up, and he had no idea how to fix it. When they reached his aging vehicle, he opened the trunk and handed over the shopping bags.

"Camille—"

"Baylor—"

They spoke simultaneously, halted, laughed self-consciously.

"I'm sorry I spoiled dinner," she said, staring at the toes of her shoes.

"It wasn't spoiled, exactly," he said. "In fact, I found the evening . . . interesting."

"Right. Risking your life for someone you hardly know is much preferable to a quiet bowl of clam chowder."

He found himself laughing. That was the first time she'd shown him her sense of humor. He liked it. He liked her. Just the same, this time when she stuck her arm through the handle of her shopping bag and extended it for a farewell handshake, he took it, though he was surprisingly reluctant to say goodbye to her.

"No hard feelings?" she said.

In reply he pulled her closer, leaned down and brushed his lips over hers. He hadn't planned to kiss her; it just happened. When she froze, staring up at him with wide, surprised eyes, he took advantage of her immobility and kissed her again, harder.

All at once her hesitant lips came alive under his, as though she'd been plugged into a live socket. Both shopping bags thunked to the pavement and she wrapped her arms around him like an affectionate vine. His hands became tangled in her soft brown hair, nudging her hat until it slipped off. All the while he kissed her as if he'd been born to do nothing else.

Only when a passing motorist honked did they come to their senses. Camille struggled to free herself from the embrace, and Baylor reluctantly released her.

"Holy Mary Mother of God," she said all in a rush, staring up at him as if he'd grown a second head. Then without another word she snatched up her possessions and strode away with the haughtiness of a princess.

"You're just full of surprises, aren't you, Camille," he murmured as he watched her retreating silhouette. He had to stifle an urge to call after her. That unexpected kiss had affected him more profoundly than he cared to admit.

Keeping careful track of her retreat, he started his car and drove to the parking lot cashier's box, where he paid a ridiculous sum for the small spot of pavement his car had occupied all day. Then he pulled out of the lot and around a corner, never losing sight of the neon dress and blue hat. Remembering how easily she'd spotted him this morning, he kept well back.

She rounded a corner and was out of his line of vision for almost a minute. When he turned the corner himself, it took him several moments to spot her. She was sitting in a doorway—a young, fashionably dressed bag lady. It suddenly occurred to Baylor that she had no place to go. She'd probably checked out of her hotel this morning, and now, with no money, she was out on the street.

It was a cinch he couldn't leave her there. No matter what crime she'd committed, she didn't deserve to be left at the mercy of the city elements at night. He pulled up to the curb and rolled down the passenger window. "Hey, lady, lookin' for a good time?"

Camille jerked her head up as panic zinged through her body, until she recognized the car and the man calling to her. After that sizzling kiss, she'd wanted to be as far away from him as possible. His obvious desire for her was intimidating, her own response was absolutely terrifying. She'd had no idea her physical awareness of a man could be so intense and uncontrollable.

Now, however, she was relieved beyond words to see him. Five minutes of contemplating a cold night on a park bench had changed her outlook completely. Right now he was her only ally in this whole monstrous town, and she'd be crazy to rebuke his friendliness.

She sauntered to his car and leaned through the window. "Are you offering a good time?" she inquired in kind, eyebrows raised, surprised at her own ability to engage in this type of senseless banter, surprised even further that she found it kind of fun.

His expression turned serious. "You don't have a hotel, do you." It was a statement, not a question.

She shook her head.

"Get in," he ordered. "You are sadly lacking in survival instinct."

She opened the back door and thrust her shopping bags onto the seat, then climbed into the front. "That's funny. Paul used to say that to me all the time."

"I'm not surprised."

Oddly enough, the criticism didn't bother her coming from Baylor. She deserved it, after all. "I don't suppose you'd care to lend me enough money for a hotel room, would you? It doesn't have to be anything fancy."

"Nope."

"Not even the YWCA?" she asked hopefully. "I'll pay you back tomorrow."

"Nope. No hotels. You're coming home with me."

Chapter Three

Camille leaned back against the cracked leather interior of the old car and sighed audibly. She knew she shouldn't be so relieved. She'd just agreed to spend the night with a man she barely knew.

She could almost hear Nita's chastising voice, telling her she was making a grave mistake. Paul's conservative secretary had very definite ideas about the "proper conduct" between men and women, and she didn't hesitate to air them. She'd also warned Camille on numerous occasions about trusting strangers.

But this situation was different, Camille told herself. Baylor wasn't exactly a stranger. She'd spent the day with him, more or less, although to be truthful she knew very little about him. Still, he'd offered help when she needed it, and he'd risked his life for her. She also knew his kiss could make steam blow out of her ears. Could she call a man a stranger after he'd kissed her?

The memory of that kiss gave her a prickle of apprehension. Maybe it wasn't wise for her to spend the night under the same roof with a man who caused such an extreme hormonal reaction. Was it too late for her to change her mind and insist on a hotel? But the thought of again facing the city alone wasn't at all appealing.

In the end she tamped down her apprehension and let Baylor take her home. She knew with unwavering certainty that she had nothing to fear from him. Her own desires posed the biggest threat, and surely she could control a few measly hormones.

It was a short drive to Charlestown, just across the Washington Avenue bridge. The sight of Inner Boston Harbor at night, with its ships nestled in their berths and its sailboats bobbing contentedly, sent another wave of longing over Camille. What must it feel like to board one of those boats and sail off to exotic ports? She'd like to go on a cruise someday, she decided, though right now she had her hands full with her current adventure.

"Have you ever traveled on a ship?" she asked Baylor impulsively, glad for a nice, neutral topic of conversation.

He smiled, though he never took his eyes off the treacherous traffic. "Once, when I was a kid. My father had some business to take care of in Switzerland, and he decided to make a family vacation out of it. We did the transatlantic number on the old *Queen Elizabeth*."

She sighed elaborately. "Was it wonderful?"

"No. I was seasick for five days straight. By the time I got my sea legs, the ship was pulling into Southampton."

She wrinkled her nose, remembering her own bouts of motion sickness as a child. "What did your father do in Switzerland?"

"Oh, he gave a talk, I suppose. He's an engineer."

"What sort of engineer?" Camille persisted, sensing a certain reluctance in Baylor but too curious to curb her questions.

"Mechanical. He invents things, most notably a little gizmo used in hospitals to analyze blood samples."

"That's fascinating." She wondered if Baylor's father was a wealthy man. Medical inventions could yield millions for their creators. On the other hand, people like herself and Paul, who worked for a corporation, couldn't hope for much more than a healthy raise in salary if and when their inventions hit pay dirt. Of course, she hadn't chosen her profession to become rich. In fact, she hadn't chosen it at all. Her well-meaning parents had chosen it for her.

"Was it fun, growing up with an inventor?" she asked.

"Yeah, I guess it was," he answered, drawing out the sentence. "Some of my best toys came out of his workshop, made from leftover junk. I've always envied that special talent he has to make something out of nothing."

Camille detected a certain ambivalence in Baylor's voice that bothered her—as if talking about his father made him both proud and ashamed. Whatever it was, she decided not to pursue the subject further. If she kept up these questions, Baylor was bound to reciprocate with queries of his own. She didn't want to tell him about her own profession. It was too soon.

"Are we driving around in circles?" she asked instead. Although her sense of direction was subject to severe malfunction, she could have sworn they'd passed Cluny's Bakery before.

"I'm looking for a parking place."

"You live here?" She studied the steep, narrow street with a keen eye.

"Right over the Irish pub, which makes parking in the evening a trifle tricky—aha! Gotcha." Almost before Camille was aware that another car was pulling away from the curb, Baylor had swung the sedan into the empty space in one smooth movement.

"That must take practice," she marveled as they climbed out of the car.

"Years' worth."

"You've lived here a while, then?"

He opened the back door and pulled out her shopping bags. "More than ten years."

"Where did you live before?" She knew she was asking too many questions again.

"Texas. Waco, Texas."

"Ah, Baylor University." One of dozens of schools that had tried to attract her to their graduate programs. Such attempts had been futile, of course. Even if another school had offered a program superior to MIT's, she couldn't have moved away from her parents. "You must be pretty important if they named a school after you."

He smiled at her attempted humor. "I'm afraid you've got it backward. My father is a bit extreme when it comes to showing loyalty to his alma mater."

"You don't have a Texas drawl," she noted.

"I used to. I've lost it, strictly as a defense mechanism. Used to be every time I opened my mouth, some native Bostonian would split a gut."

"Split a gut?" she repeated, confused.

"Laugh at me. Excessively." He ducked into a narrow passage. "This way."

Camille followed him through a dark alley full of questionable odors and experienced a moment of trepidation. What sort of accommodations had she let herself in for? But all of her concerns melted when they reached the top of the spiral staircase and Baylor opened his front door. A single, green-glassed lamp suspended from the ceiling revealed the warmest, most inviting living space she'd ever seen.

"What a great place," she said with unabashed sincerity, strolling into the middle of the living room and twirling around to take it all in. The room was long and narrow, but the high ceilings and a large window facing the street gave it a feeling of openness. One wall was exposed red brick, covered with an array of framed prints, photos, and knotty abstract wall hangings. The floors were pale, glossy wood, with several Oriental carpets thrown about here and there, showing varying degrees of wear. The furniture was not new, but the oatmeal-colored cushions looked plump and soft and altogether inviting.

"You really like it?" he asked, seemingly pleased with her appraisal.

She nodded enthusiastically.

"My mother said, on the occasion of her one and only visit here, that it looked as if I'd furnished it from garage sales."

Camille shook her head in denial. How could anyone fail to see the charm and personality of this place? It made her austere quarters at Easterwood look as inviting as a hospital room. "It's wonderful. Show me the rest."

He obliged her by taking her around a low wall made of glass blocks and through an efficient gray and white kitchen, then back to a tiny but intricately tiled bathroom, and finally to the bedroom.

The one bedroom.

He set her shopping bags onto the floor. "I'll get some fresh sheets," he said casually, opening a closet door.

Camille felt her legs quivering beneath her. She edged her way to the modern pedestal bed and sank onto a corner of it, her mind racing with possibilities.

Did Baylor expect her to sleep with him? The thought sent a wave of jitters from the pit of her stomach outward, and she fervently wished she had some frame of reference for how to behave in such a situation. She knew everything there was to know about the biological aspects of sex, but next to nothing about the social niceties connected with it. Why hadn't she bothered to find out these things?

She focused her eyes on Baylor's broad-shouldered back. How would it feel to run her hands along those firm muscles? She was amazed that such a thought would even enter her head. She'd never stroked a man's back before.

"I'm trying to find some sheets that match," he said, still rifling through the contents of the cluttered closet. "I don't have overnight guests too often."

Thank heavens for that, she thought, grateful that she wasn't the latest in a long string of sleep-over companions.

"Ah, here we go." He turned toward her with an armload of paisley sheets, still in their store wrapping. "They were a gift. Pretty, but not quite my style."

"Pretty," she agreed as she pictured herself sleeping against the brightly colored paisleys. She shook her head to dispel the image when she realized that her imagination had conjured up Baylor sleeping beside her. "I . . . um, would it be all right if I took a bath?"

"Sure. I suppose you might like some pajamas, too."

"Actually I have a—" She stopped, remembering the slinky bits of silk she'd been talked into buying at a Newbury Street boutique earlier that day. "I'd love some pajamas."

Five minutes later Camille was reclining up to her neck in steaming water, but the heat seeping into her tired body did little to relax her as doubt after doubt assailed her vulnerable mind. What was she doing here? Twenty-four hours ago she'd never imagined herself in such a dilemma. Sure, she'd wanted to experience life to its fullest, but she simply wasn't prepared to live this fully, this fast.

When she at last climbed out of the tub, having bought herself as much time as she dared without rousing Baylor's concern, she found a pair of powder blue pajamas waiting for her on the edge of the sink. She wondered vaguely how they'd gotten there. They smelled new, and she figured they were probably a gift, as the sheets were—and also not Baylor's style. He seemed the type to sleep in the nude, though she had no idea what had drawn her to that conclusion.

The pajamas swallowed her whole. With the legs and sleeves rolled up, the getup was only slightly less ridiculous-looking, but at least she was modestly covered. She took a deep breath and opened the door, prepared to confront head-on this business of sleeping arrangements, if necessary. She hoped the unappealing sight of her in baggy pajamas would negate the need for her to say anything.

She padded quietly to the bedroom. The bed was now clothed in the paisley sheets, but thankfully Baylor wasn't among them.

She located him a few moments later, seated at a small marble-top table in the dining area, bent over a magazine. His shirt was unbuttoned, revealing a thin, snow-white undershirt that was somehow more unnerving than bare chest would have been.

He looked up at her and grinned, apparently finding her costume just as silly-looking as she had. "Feel better?" he asked.

"Much. Listen, Baylor," she began in her most no-nonsense tone of voice, "I'd like to straighten something out."

His brows drew together in concern at her grave tone. "Is something wrong?"

She tried to hold his gaze but found she couldn't. Her eyes strayed—and that's when she saw the couch, made up with sheets, blanket and pillows.

She felt like an utter fool.

"Camille?"

"I, um, what I meant was..." *Think, silly. Say something.* "I don't want to sleep in your bed." *Brilliant.* "I mean, I feel bad putting you out of your bed. Let me sleep on the couch."

He stared at her without speaking for a moment, causing her to feel more and more foolish. Here she'd been so sure Baylor had seduction on his mind, when all the while he'd planned to sleep on the couch. How unsophisticated could she be? And why hadn't he made his intentions clear from the beginning and saved her all this needless agonizing?

Baylor tried to read her mood, but she was giving out mixed signals. Her breathing was rapid, and she was twisting her fingers around themselves nervously, yet her warm hazel eyes reflected a definite expression of relief... or was it disappointment?

It occurred to him then that she might be apprehensive about spending the night with him. Did she think he planned to seduce her? he thought, acknowledging that the idea had a certain appeal.

"You're my guest," he finally said, wanting to put her at ease. "I don't mind the couch. I can fall asleep anywhere. Please, take the bed."

She hesitated a moment. "All right, if you're sure. Um, what are you reading?"

He welcomed the change in subject. "It's a crossword puzzle. A brutal one, as a matter of fact. I've been at it for days, but I think I'm ready to admit I'm stumped."

"Want me to try? I love crosswords, though I haven't worked on one in a few years."

He slid the magazine across the table toward her as she pulled up a chair. "Sure, take a shot at it," he said smugly. He'd been doing crosswords his whole life, having picked up the habit from his father. Although he'd never achieve his father's skill, he'd advanced through hundreds of puzzles with sheer, dogged determination until he'd reached an enviable level of expertise. Genius or not, he doubted Camille could crack this one.

Again, however, he'd underestimated her. She stared silently at the puzzle for about five minutes, after which she picked up his pencil and began to fill in squares. "You made a little mistake," she commented casually as she made an erasure. "That's how you got fouled up." She wrote in a few more answers, then handed the almost-completed puzzle back to him. "There, I think you can handle it from here."

"Thanks," he mumbled, taking back the magazine, then pushing it aside. He was irritated beyond reason that she could solve the puzzle with so little effort. Then an idea occurred to him. "It's still early. Would you like to work on another puzzle? I have books full of them."

Her face lit up with an eager smile as she nodded assent. "Puzzles are so relaxing. I used to do them when I couldn't sleep."

Funny, puzzles had the exact opposite effect on him, Baylor thought as he scanned his bookshelf. They tended to put him on edge. He flipped through several magazines and booklets until he found the one he wanted. *Killer Crosswords*. He'd never been able to solve more than a couple of clues on any of these. He opened the booklet to a fresh puzzle and handed it to her with a confident flourish. "This should keep you busy for a while."

She gave him a sedate nod as she took the booklet.

Baylor chose a book of expert mazes for himself. Word puzzles made him edgy, but mazes had a soothing effect.

Thirty minutes later, Camille cleared her throat to get his attention, then handed him the *Killer Crosswords* book. "That was a tough one," she said. The puzzle was completed, with not a single sign of eraser marks. "What else do you have?"

Baylor was stunned. That was the hardest book he had in the house, and it was child's play to her. Maybe a mechanical puzzle would challenge her. "I don't suppose a Rubik's Cube would interest you?"

"Um, no. I figured that one out a while back." Her eyes strayed to the bookshelf, where a number of other three-dimensional puzzles were displayed. After awarding each one a quick study, she stood and moved toward a foot-high wooden elephant, made of hundreds of interlocking pieces. "This one looks like fun. Do you mind?"

"Be my guest."

She brought it to the table. He disassembled the teak-wood animal for her, making sure to mix up the pieces as thoroughly as possible. No sense making it any easier for her than necessary.

"What if I can't do it?" she asked, worrying her lower lip with her teeth. "Can you put it back together?"

He assured her that he could. His father had bought the elephant in India when Baylor was about twelve. It had taken him more than a week to solve the puzzle the first time, but now he could assemble the beast in his sleep.

As Camille worked, Baylor watched, though he pretended to concentrate on one of his mazes. Her long hair was drawn up in a careless ponytail on top of her head, so that the chestnut curls cascaded around her face. The sprinkling of cinnamon-colored freckles across her nose was more prominent now that her makeup was gone, emphasizing her youth and freshness. Her eyelashes cast long shadows over her cheekbones as she looked down at the puzzle. The thin cotton pajamas revealed just the barest curve of her breasts when she leaned back to think.

Baylor's stomach tightened with an unexpected rush of desire, and he made himself look away. She reminded him of a wood nymph. It was inconceivable that she was a thief. Yet Paul would never make such accusations without good reason.

He needed to talk to Paul again. He'd wait until Camille was asleep.

When next he checked her progress on the elephant, he was surprised at how little she'd gotten done. She had all four legs connected, which was better-than-average progress, but she appeared to be at a standstill. He was a little ashamed at the pleasure he derived from her frustrated expression.

"Want a clue?" he asked, struggling to keep the smugness out of his voice.

"Certainly not," she bristled. "I just need a little more time." But when she glanced up at him, almost slyly, she was grinning. "This kind of puzzle isn't my strong suit," she admitted. "But I like them, anyway."

After a few more minutes, she yawned elaborately. "I'm going to have to give up on Rumbo here and go to bed," she announced.

"Rumbo?"

"Isn't there a famous elephant named Rumbo?"

"I think you mean *Dumbo*," he explained indulgently. "There's one called 'Jumbo,' too. Then there's Rambo, but he's not an elephant."

"All right, so I'm not up on circus trivia," she said, laughing at her error. "Whatever the elephant's name is, maybe I'll receive a bolt of inspiration in the night, and I'll be able to finish him up in the morning."

"Does that really happen?" he asked, allowing his fascination with her mega-intelligence to surface. "Do you ever sleep on a problem, then wake up with the answer?"

She replied as if the question surprised her. "Lots of times. At work—at my former job—sometimes something would seem impossible late at night, but in the morning the solution would be simple."

"What did you do at your old job?" he asked, just to see what sort of answer he'd get. There was no reason she wouldn't tell him some generalities about her work, unless she had something to hide.

Their eyes met for the span of a heartbeat, as if she were on the verge of revealing something, but she looked away before that could happen. "I'd prefer not to talk about it just now," she said in a soft voice as she pushed herself away from the table.

"Why not?" he prodded, standing as she did.

One corner of her generous mouth lifted in a self-deprecating smile. "Believe me, you wouldn't find it at all interesting. But it's nice of you to ask. In fact, you've been very nice all the way around." She took a step closer to him, as if she might reach out to touch him, but something seemed to hold her back.

Nice? That was the last word he would use to describe himself at this moment, he thought as her clean, womanly scent surrounded him. A nice man wouldn't face an obviously innocent woman and mentally strip her clothes away. A nice man wouldn't dwell on thoughts of smooth ivory skin and soft, yielding breasts against his chest. . . .

She stood still as a statue for a moment more, reminding him of a frightened fawn, poised for flight. Finally she reached out and gave his forearm a lightning-quick squeeze before jerking her hand back abruptly. "Thanks again for everything," she continued, rushing the words out. "I hope that soon I'll be in a position to pay you back for all you've done."

When you've sold M23? his suspicious mind countered. Why did he continue to picture her as innocent when he knew better? "No payback is necessary," he said tersely. Remembering who she was and what she'd probably done cooled his desire. Baylor had spent too many years in law enforcement to allow himself to be intimate with a thief, no matter how enticing a thief she was. He'd seen firsthand the damage that white-collar crime could wreak on businesses and people alike.

She gave him one last, perplexed look before turning and walking toward the bedroom. Even in the gigantic pajamas she managed to appear slim and graceful, and he remembered again what it had felt like to hold her against him.

Dammit, wasn't it possible that Paul was wrong?

Baylor worked a few more mazes until more than an hour had passed—plenty of time for Camille to fall asleep. Then he moved into the kitchen and dialed Paul's familiar home number. He half expected to reach the answering machine. It was still before midnight, and Paul often worked in his dreary laboratory far into the wee hours. But he must have knocked off early, because it was Paul's live and very anxious voice that answered.

"It's me," Baylor said without preamble.

"Where have you been? Did you locate Camille?"

"I've been busy, and yes, I found her again. As a matter of fact, even as we speak she's asleep in my bedroom." An angry silence greeted that comment, so Baylor quickly clarified. "Don't worry, I haven't sullied your precious little genius. She's sleeping alone."

"Then what is going on?" Paul demanded.

"She ended up without a place to stay, so I offered her mine—it's a long story, don't even ask," he added just as Paul was about to object again. "I can keep an eye on her this way."

"I suppose so," Paul said, though his doubt was obvious. "What about the diskettes?"

"I was getting to that. The good news is she hasn't made contact with a buyer, if she has one. The bad news is . . ." he hesitated, then pressed on. "Her backpack was stolen by a teenage thug, and the disks were in it."

"Oh great glory!" Coming from Paul, who virtually never lost his temper, the mild epithet had the effect of the most obscene curse imaginable. "Are you sure the disks were in her backpack?"

"Judging from her reaction to the theft, I'd say yes. She even admitted that she'd lost something important to her."

"Is there any chance of recovering the pack?"

"I'm working on it, Paul," Baylor replied in his most soothing voice. "At least none of your competitors will get their hands on it. The kid who lifted the backpack has no way of knowing that the disks are valuable. At worst he'll simply throw them away."

Paul made a strangled sound. "And you don't think that's bad? Years' worth of work will be down the tubes. So help me, I'll see that girl in jail for the rest of her life. Don't you dare lose her again!"

Paul's change in attitude alarmed Baylor. Just this morning, Paul had sounded much more forgiving toward

Camille, believing that if she'd stolen the project, she had a good reason for doing so. Now he sounded downright vindictive.

"Paul," Baylor began cautiously, "are you absolutely sure Camille did it? I'm still having a hard time believing—"

"Yes, she did it, the ungrateful little wretch. I haven't told you the latest."

Baylor's stomach wrenched with something akin to pain. Somehow, he didn't think he wanted to hear what was coming next. "What's the latest?" he asked, gritting his teeth against the unpleasant truth.

"Project M23 entailed several physical components, in addition to the computer data. There were mechanical drawings, schematics, material samples—things that would have been too big and bulky for Camille to carry out in a backpack. Nonetheless, those things were discovered missing, too."

"I'd say that points to Camille's innocence," Baylor inserted, grabbing on to the thread of hope.

"I thought so too, until I learned something that pretty well cements the case against Camille. Yesterday morning Nita saw her headed toward the mail room with a huge package, just the right size to hold those physical components. The guys in the mail room confirm that Camille did send a package of those dimensions."

Baylor felt his insides cramping painfully as his last hopes for her innocence dwindled. No matter how strongly he was attracted to her, no matter how much he *liked* her, he couldn't change the damning facts. She appeared to be guilty as hell.

She couldn't possibly be as sweet and gentle and trusting as she pretended, he acknowledged, swallowing the bile that threatened to rise in his throat. He'd been buffaloed.

"Are you still there, Baylor?"

"Yeah, I'm here. Look, Paul, I'll stay with this thing one more day. But then I want out. You'll have to go to the police."

"The police?" He sounded horrified. "Can you imagine what would happen if word got out that the M23 data was floating around loose?"

"No I can't," Baylor retorted impatiently. "You've been too damned tight-lipped about this mysterious project of yours. But if you can't go to the police, hire a private detective. After tomorrow I'm out." He slammed down the receiver, knowing even as he did it that he shouldn't be taking out his anger on Paul. It was Camille he was angry with—Camille, with her fawn's eyes and her unconsciously pouty lips and her gentle way of moving. Camille, with her dangerously deceptive innocence, who had just confirmed his worst nightmare.

He'd lost his instinct, the one thing upon which his entire career on the police force had relied.

He'd once considered himself an expert at reading people. His instinct told him when someone was lying, when they were guilty or innocent, when they were bluffing or dead serious. He'd had the uncanny ability to assess a person, a crime scene or a police report, and magically come up with the right answers.

His gut kept telling him Camille couldn't be a criminal, yet cold facts dictated otherwise. Obviously his instinct was failing him—again.

His mind recoiled as the memory of the tense hostage situation jumped into focus despite his attempts to push it back. Once again he could smell the fear and feel the stinging snow blowing against the back of his neck just as it had been that late night two months ago. He could see every detail of the rundown neighborhood where a drunken man had held his wife and child hostage with a loaded Saturday-night-special. He remembered precisely what it felt like to make that split-second decision. He could still hear the crack and the moments of profound silence afterward. He could still see blood in the snow....

Camille pulled herself back into the bedroom and silently closed the door, her heart pounding in her ears. Baylor had been talking to Paul.

She hadn't intended to eavesdrop. She'd been lying awake in Baylor's oversized bed, unable to come even close to sleeping. Insomnia had long been a companion of hers, striking whenever she was worried or unsettled. She should have gone to bed after the first puzzle, instead of concentrating so hard on that blasted elephant.

But it wasn't just the elephant's mystery that had kept her tossing restlessly. Something about Baylor's manner had been bothering her.

She was beginning to wonder if she'd been foolish after all, suspecting Baylor's intent. Though he'd behaved the perfect gentleman all evening, more than once she'd felt his eyes on her. And just before she'd gone to bed, when she'd touched him so fleetingly, he'd looked as if he wanted to eat her alive. He wasn't indifferent to her. Even with her meager experience, she had that much figured out.

The memory of that innocent touch of her hand to his arm did little to relax her mind or her body. She'd made a mistake, coming so close to him when she'd sensed the sexual vibrations in the air. As soon as her hand had come in contact with his sleeve, she'd been treated to a bolt of awareness, the same as when the last connection is made in an electrical circuit. What would have happened if she'd touched bare skin? Or if she'd leaned up to kiss him, as her wild impulses had directed? Her hormones were much more difficult to control than she'd imagined.

She was still staring at the ceiling, wide awake, as midnight approached. That's when she'd heard Baylor's voice. Concerned that something was wrong, she'd gotten out of bed and tiptoed into the hallway, breathing a sigh of relief as she realized he was only talking on the phone. She'd been about to retreat when she'd heard her own name.

Rooted to the spot where she stood, she'd listened, determined to find out who in the world he might be discussing her with. Immediately she'd heard Paul's name, and she'd known an anger so hot and turbulent she'd nearly shrieked with it.

Damn Baylor Pierce for being a sneaking, double-crossing liar! He'd been Paul's envoy all along, pretending an interest in her for...for what? She stilled her roiling thoughts and listened again. Why was he telling Paul about her *backpack*, for pity's sake? Was her former boss merely concerned about her?

She thought not. There was something sinister about this conversation in the dark of night, about this whole situation, as a matter of fact. As though Paul and Baylor were conspiring against her.

The more she listened, the less sense she made of the one-sided conversation. All this talk about diskettes— surely not *her* diskettes—and the police made her nervous. Who would want her computer diskettes? Was Paul trying to intimate that she'd made off with Easterwood property? If so, he wouldn't get very far. She'd always kept her personal notes on diskettes purchased at the employee commissary with her own money.

Maybe she was jumping to conclusions, she cautioned herself. Baylor and Paul might be talking about something else altogether. Whatever it was, Baylor had clearly

been angry. He'd slammed down the receiver at the conclusion of the call.

She would have to confront Baylor and demand to know
what was going on. Then again, maybe she didn't want to
know. She felt an overwhelming need to be away from this
apartment, away from a puzzling man who had her more
turned around and confused than any wooden elephant
could. He'd been dishonest from the beginning, and all her
assumptions about him had been wildly off target.

She should have heeded Nita's advice about trusting
strangers.

Whatever Baylor's interest in her, and/or her backpack, it wasn't the healthy, sexual interest she'd been vis-
ualizing. That, she was afraid, had been just an
inexperienced woman's wishful thinking.

Chapter Four

Through sheer force of will, Camille made herself fall asleep. As anxious as she was to be gone, she also had to be practical. Her body and her brain couldn't function at peak performance without at least a few hours of rest.

Her internal alarm clock woke her at precisely five a.m., as she'd planned. Instantly alert, she slipped out of bed and fished around in her shopping bags for jeans and a sweater. She couldn't find her bra without switching on a light, so she went without. She had a feeling that today's activities would demand comfort rather than high fashion, anyway.

The bathroom mirror told her she'd lost yesterday's glamorous veneer. Restless sleep had reduced her bouncy curls to limp waves. Undaunted, she quickly brushed the long tresses, then pulled them into a loose ponytail and tied it with a scarf. The results were less than satisfying.

The pink paper sack of cosmetics from the beauty salon caught her eye. Glancing at her watch, she decided she had at least five spare minutes in which to experiment...a little mascara, a bit of liner, a touch of brow pencil, some blusher, and a dab of lip gloss. When she was done, she appraised herself critically in the mirror, satisfied that at least part of the salon's magical transformation had stayed with her. She didn't look half-bad.

Not that it really mattered. The Dawgs doubtless wouldn't give a hoot what she looked like, and Baylor wasn't likely to lay eyes on her again—not if she could help it.

With her shopping bags in tow, she crept past the kitchen and into the living room, where Baylor was asleep on the sofa, sprawled on his stomach. A pale blue blanket only half-covered him. Camille stared at him, her eyes transfixed by his pleasingly sculpted male form, faintly illuminated by the predawn light. She couldn't take her eyes off him. The thin blanket wrapped so tightly about him revealed more than it concealed of his muscular thighs and buttocks.

She forced herself to look away. Her eyes rested for a moment on his clothes, draped neatly over the back of a chair, then returned unwillingly to the man. He must be very nearly naked under that blanket, she realized with a surge of unwelcome excitement.

He moved in his sleep, rolling onto his side and cradling his head against his arm. Camille's hand flew to her mouth to stifle a gasp as he kicked more of the covers aside, revealing his flat, taught abdomen. Good Lord, he wasn't just *nearly* naked. The man slept in the nude, and only a fortuitously positioned corner of the blanket prevented Camille from seeing the rest of his anatomy.

She flushed guiltily. How Baylor slept was his business. He had no reason to suspect that his houseguest would be prowling around in the wee hours of the morning, so he had no reason to be thinking of modesty.

He could awaken at any moment—she had to get out of there. Baylor's wallet sat on the coffee table next to a handful of change. She opened the wallet and counted the bills—twenty-eight dollars. After a moment's deliberation, she took twenty and stuffed it into her pocket, along with a few quarters. She was only borrowing the money, she told herself. As soon as she got her life straightened out, she'd pay him back.

She started for the door, then paused. She ought to leave him a note, though he didn't really deserve such consideration after all the deception he'd dealt her. Still, he'd provided her dinner and given her a place to sleep, for which she was grateful.

She stepped noiselessly to the kitchen, where she remembered seeing a pad and pencil by the phone. She scribbled out a quick message without benefit of any light and left it on the table before quietly exiting and shutting the door behind her.

A series of unfamiliar stimuli gently prodded Baylor awake: soft footsteps, the click of his front door dead bolt, a gust of cold air, and the lingering, fresh scent of a woman. He stretched and rubbed his eyes, trying to put it all together. Then he remembered Camille, and his eyes flew open as a rush of awareness hit him. She'd been here, in this room, while he slept. He knew it.

Immediately he was fully awake. He wrapped the blanket around his waist and strode purposefully toward the bedroom, knowing what he would find and dreading it all the same. When he flipped on the light, he saw that the bed was empty. So was the bathroom. Her shopping bags were gone.

But she couldn't be far, he realized as he let the blanket drop. Her exit was what had awakened him. He might be able to catch her.

He returned to the bedroom and opened a dresser drawer. With lightning speed he pulled on briefs, jeans, a sweatshirt and running shoes, omitting socks in his haste. He sprinted the length of his apartment and out the door, not bothering to lock it. He raced down the stairs and onto the street. Gazing left, right, and left again, he squinted into the cold, predawn drizzle for some sign of her. But the sidewalks were deserted.

A string of colorful curses echoed through the silent alley as Baylor stomped back up the spiral staircase. The little genius had outfoxed him again.

As he dialed Paul's number he found the note Camille had left:

Baylor, I borrowed $20 and some change, plus a pair of socks. I'll return both. Please don't follow me again. Whatever it is you and Paul have cooked up, forget it. Just leave me alone.

Baylor hung up the phone before the connection was made, disturbed over the unsigned note. The animosity it contained stung him. What had happened to turn last night's warm gratitude into this morning's cold brush-off?

After a moment the answer was glaringly apparent. Camille had overheard his conversation with Paul. She knew they were onto her. Her abrupt departure was just one more indication of her guilt.

He ought to be furious with her, but for some reason he wasn't. Maybe it was the tone of the note, which sounded as if she felt hurt or betrayed rather than clever. Maybe it was the fact that she'd promised to return a measly twenty dollars and a pair of socks. What felonious thief would make such a gesture?

He glanced at his watch, noting that it wasn't yet six. With a sadistic smile he dialed Paul's number again. Paul was a notoriously late riser, but why should he be allowed to slumber peacefully when Baylor was so agonizingly awake?

"She gave me the slip again," he said when Paul answered the phone with a groggy croak.

"What? Lord, Baylor, I thought you were a detective."

"Former detective. And you're wasting your time if you're trying to make me feel stupid, because I couldn't feel any stupider."

"For heaven's sake, man, why are you wasting time calling me? Find her!"

"Wouldn't you rather me find her backpack?" Baylor asked carefully.

"Find one and you'll find the other. She's probably out looking for those computer disks right now." Paul hung up, but his last words echoed in Baylor's mind, giving him chills. That's why Camille had left here so early—to get a head start on him. Without any trepidation she'd find those punk thugs and demand the return of her things, as she had last night. Genius or no, the little fool might get herself into some serious trouble.

There was only one course of action Baylor could take, and that was to get to the Dawgs before she did.

Camille sat in a tiny bakery not four blocks from Baylor's apartment, daintily nibbling on a cruller. Just a few minutes earlier she'd used the pay phone on the wall to call Larry Buford, one of Easterwood's high-level technicians and the only person she knew who could outmaneuver her on a computer. Ordinarily Larry wouldn't give her the time of day. But not long ago she'd inadvertently walked in on him when he was in the process of "fixing" a few parking tickets—after having hacked his way into the Boston Police Department computer system. Chagrined, he'd promised to do her a favor someday if she'd just keep her mouth shut about his indiscretion. Now she was calling in that favor.

Larry had sounded sleepy and surprised to hear from her. "Are you feeling better?" he asked politely.

"Better than what?"

He was silent a moment. "Paul said you had a bad case of the flu."

"Oh, for Pete's sake, why does everything have to be so cloak-and-dagger? I'm not sick. I quit."

Larry was silent for another moment. Finally he asked in a hushed tone. "Who hired you away?"

"No one! I'd never work for another company. I just had to get out of there."

"Why?"

"I'll discuss it at length another time, Larry," she said with an impatient sigh. "Right now I have a problem, and I need that favor you owe me." She'd decided last night that she would pursue her backpack on her own. Aside from wanting her notes and her traveler's checks, she had to know why Paul and Baylor were interested in her personal possessions. And she'd never find out unless she recovered the pack first. "Can you break into the police department computer for me?" she asked in a casual voice.

"Don't tell me *you* got parking tickets," Larry said, snickering. "I didn't think you knew how to drive."

She didn't, a further reminder that her former life had been a laughably narrow existence. "I don't want you to tamper with anything," she bristled. "I just want some information on a teenage gang called the Dawgs. I'm trying to locate one of their members who...has something of mine."

"Sure, I'll give it a try," Larry had agreed. "Where can I call you back?"

She'd given him the pay phone's number, then sat down to wait.

When she finished the cruller, she bought a second one, got a refill on her coffee, then waited some more while the bakery cashier kept a wary eye on her. She paged through a newspaper, and when she was done she simply gazed out the window at a cold, penetrating drizzle, a far cry from yesterday's springlike temperatures. The morning rush hour crowd came and went.

Finally, at almost nine o'clock, the pay phone rang and Camille jumped to answer it.

"There's a lot of information on the Dawgs," Larry said without preamble. "It appears that they're Boston's latest threat to law and order. Got a pen?"

She didn't, but she could remember what she needed. Near-perfect recall came in handy sometimes.

In the next five minutes she learned a lot about her adversaries. The gang members had been arrested for a host of mostly minor crimes, from possession of illegal weapons to vandalism to larceny, but only one of them had ever been in serious trouble. His name was Milo Sawyer.

"I'd watch out for that dude," Larry warned. "He's been charged with armed robbery. He's out on bond right now, awaiting trial."

"I'm not interested in him," said Camille. "I'm looking for an Asian boy."

"Oh. Let's see, I think there's one...yeah. In-Ho Nguyen. That's the only Asian-sounding name on the list of known members. He's no picnic, either. He's only seventeen, and he's already served time at the juvenile detention center for stealing a car. He's out on parole."

"In-Ho Nguyen," Camille murmured, filing the name away for future reference. "Is there an address?"

Larry gave her a street and number in Chinatown, which she also stored in her mental file cabinet.

Finally Larry had information about the Dawgs' hangout. "They tend to roam all over the city," he said. "But their official turf is loosely around the Navy Yard, and they've been known to collect at any of several abandoned warehouses down there."

"Thanks, Larry. You're amazing."

"I'm also late for work," he said, obviously irritated.

"Oh, yes, about work. Please don't tell anyone you talked to me."

"Now who's playing cloak-and-dagger?"

"I know it's silly. But you won't say anything, will you?"

"I'll keep quiet. But you'll owe me again."

"Fine, fine," Camille agreed quickly before she said goodbye. Now at least she knew who she was looking for and where to start the hunt. But Baylor had access to the same computer Larry had sneaked into, she reminded herself. He might be way ahead of her. She put another dime into the phone and called a taxi, which arrived less than five minutes later.

"Where to?" the driver asked.

"About how much will it cost to get to the Navy Yard?" she asked as she climbed inside the taxi, mindful of the sixteen or so dollars she had left of Baylor's twenty.

The cabbie laughed. "About two bucks. You're almost there now."

That was good news. She leaned back in her seat and thought about what she'd say to the Dawgs when she found them. A soft, sympathetic approach would be best, she decided. They were just kids, after all, and all kids were basically insecure. They painted graffiti on walls and stole cars for the notoriety it got them. Somehow, she'd appeal to that need for attention.

"Is this really where you want to go?" the driver asked.

Camille took a good look at her surroundings and shivered. In the damp gray mist, the quiet Navy Yard looked particularly foreboding. Even the tall masts of the USS *Constitution*, silhouetted against a gunmetal-gray sky, seemed sinister.

"I'm looking for an abandoned warehouse," said Camille.

"Any particular one?" the cabbie said, his words followed by a snort of disdain.

"I'll know it when I see it," she hedged, reluctant to wander about this neighborhood alone. "Could we just . . . drive around a bit?"

"Sure, why not?" he agreed. "It's your nickel."

The taxi putted past the *Constitution*, where a line of tourists was forming to board the old frigate, and then made its way up and down a series of crooked streets. Each time Camille saw a building that even remotely resembled a warehouse, she peered intently at it, but she saw nothing that would indicate the Dawgs' presence.

Maybe this wasn't such a wise idea after all, she thought as the cab passed two unsavory looking men, leaning against a wall and sharing a bottle of something. Maybe she should just direct the cab driver to her bank, where she could replace her traveler's checks and start over, as if yesterday had never happened. She was on the verge of making this decision when she spotted two green fatigue jackets on two slender young men slouching in a doorway.

"Stop here," she told the driver.

"Here? I . . . I don't know about this. Are you meeting someone?"

"Those two kids in the doorway. How much do I owe?"

"You must be nuts!" The driver turned to stare at her over his shoulder. "Those punks belong to the Dawgs. You don't want to mess with them. You shoulda seen what they did to my cab a coupla months ago. Four hundred dollars worth of damage, and all I did was—"

"Yes, yes, I understand," she said impatiently. "How much do I owe?"

He shrugged. "It's your hide. Personally those Dawgs give me the willies. The fare comes to six-twenty-five."

She paid him in exact change, automatically adding a precise tip, then grabbed her cumbersome shopping bags and got out.

The cabbie opened his window. "You don't want me to wait, do you?"

Camille took one more look at the two teenagers, with their ripped jeans and dirty faces and grim expressions. They were only fifteen or sixteen, but even so they were bigger than she was. "As a matter of fact . . ."

"I didn't think so," the cabbie said quickly before speeding off, leaving a cloud of exhaust in his wake.

Well, she was in the thick of it now, she thought with a sigh of resignation. She might as well do what she came here to do. Purposefully she approached the two youths, who glared suspiciously at her as she drew closer. She gave them what she hoped was a warm smile. They responded by visually examining her from head to toe, as if she were a prize heifer on the auction block.

She didn't recognize these two. She didn't think they'd been with the group last night. "Hello," she ventured in an unsteady voice. "I'm looking for someone. Maybe you boys could help me out."

"Did you hear that, Eddie?" one asked the other. "She called us 'boys.' We're *men*, chicky."

Camille's smile vanished as she nervously cleared her throat. "My mistake." So much for a soft approach. "I'm looking for In-Ho Nguyen. He has something I want."

"Oooooh." The boy leaned uncomfortably close to her. "Maybe I have something you want."

"I doubt that," she said with an involuntary grimace. "Can you tell me where to find In-Ho? There might be a reward in it for you," she added.

The boy who had appointed himself as spokesman turned to the one he'd called Eddie. "A reward!" he exclaimed, pretending to be impressed. He returned his attention to Camille. "You gonna give us a medal for doin' a good deed?"

She struggled to hold on to her temper. She'd had no idea any mere child could be so rude, or so intimidating. "I'm talking cash," she said evenly.

That seemed to do the trick. "Eddie, go find In-Ho and bring him to headquarters. He's hangin' out with Milo somewhere. Tell him I got a present for him."

"Sure thing," Eddie said, loping off.

"Tell him to bring the backpack," Camille called after him.

"You come with me," the other boy said to her.

She shrugged and followed him up the sidewalk, wondering just what sort of trouble she was getting herself into. The mention of Milo's name was an unwelcome surprise.

"Why is everyone so concerned about the Dawgs?" Baylor asked his former partner, Chris Fletcher. "You say they don't seem to be tied to many serious crimes."

The two men were seated in the precinct office where Baylor used to work, wrestling with a computer that didn't want to cooperate.

"They're unusual in that they don't come from one particular area. The gang's leaders handpick the members from all over, so they represent varying socioeconomic groups, varying ethnic persuasions. This gives them a wide power base." Chris had obviously done his homework. "They're not interested in fighting over turf," he continued. "In fact, they don't concern themselves with other gangs at all. They're unusually well organized, operating much in the way of a miniature syndicate."

"That does sound weird," Baylor said as he tried once again to call up the information he wanted on the computer. "Why does this thing keep freezing up on me?"

A patrolman walking through the office answered Baylor's question. "There was a breech in security earlier this morning. Someone from the outside cracked the access code. The computer's out of commission for a while, till the data processing people can figure out how to plug up the hole."

Baylor groaned. He'd have given ten-to-one odds he knew who the mysterious hacker was. "I better go with what I have," he told Chris. "Time might be more critical than I thought."

"Hey, it's good to see your ugly mug back in here," Chris said as Baylor slung his arms into the sleeves of a denim jacket. "You thinking of paying any regular visits?"

"I'm thinking about a lot of things," Baylor said in response to the loaded question. "See ya." He escaped before Chris could ask anything more personal.

It took Baylor less than ten minutes to get to the old waterfront warehouse Chris had told him about. He cruised slowly past, eyeing the grim brick building for signs of occupation. The first floor windows and doors were boarded up. Dead weeds stood three feet tall all around it.

He parked his car around a corner and got out, tucking his service revolver into the waistband of his jeans. Technically he wasn't even supposed to have a gun, much less carry it around. But his captain had refused to take back the weapon when Baylor had announced he was leaving the force. "You'll be wanting it before long," the gruff old man had assured Baylor. Turned out he'd been right.

Baylor flipped up his jacket collar as he sauntered past the warehouse. When he was sure no one was looking, he darted into the alley and around to the back of the building, where he could investigate with little chance of being spotted.

The three-story structure sat right on the water. A gigantic pulley system was once used to haul goods off barges and into the storage areas through huge bay doors. Now it stood rusted and useless, its rotting ropes in tatters.

Baylor was checking the boarded-up windows when he heard a voice, floating downward from one of the upper floors. At least, he thought it was a voice. It might have just been the wind. He tensed and listened. There it was again. A female voice. A *frightened* female voice.

A burst of adrenaline surged through Baylor's veins as his body jerked into action. Finding no means of access on the first floor, he used the pulley framework as a ladder and climbed as far as the second level. The voices were clearer now, coming from a crack in the bay door. Baylor inched his way along the second-floor ledge until he found a broken window to peek through.

In an instant he assessed the situation, and his mouth went dry. Camille was there, seated cross-legged on the floor. She looked plenty scared, her face pale and her eyes huge, but otherwise she appeared unharmed. Four gang members were with her. Two of them he didn't recognize, but one of them was the teenager who'd stolen the backpack, and the other was the kid with white hair—Milo, one of the other boys had called him. He was giving Camille a hard time, paying her back in spades for womping him with her shoe.

The backpack in question sat in the middle of the floor. Milo was pacing circles around it, pointing to it and shooting questions at Camille. Camille alternately nodded, then shook her head.

Quickly Baylor went over his options. Four of them and one of him—bad odds. He had a gun, but God only knew what kinds of weapons they might have concealed. Knives, at the very least. Despite the uncomfortably cold wind, he broke out in a sweat.

His biggest ally would be surprise. There appeared to be only one avenue of entry, and that was the huge bay door that was already open a crack. He worked his way around to that opening, taking mincing steps along the narrow, crumbling ledge and trying not to think about the black, freezing water below him. His heart hammered inside his chest at a frantic pace and his gut twisted itself into a painful knot. The bodily stress—physiological reactions to fear—were like an old friend, come to visit after a long absence.

From his new vantage point, Baylor could hear more of what went on inside. Milo was pulling items out of the backpack, one at a time, and holding them in Camille's face.

"Could this be what you're so interested in?" he asked, waving a thick wallet of traveler's checks.

She stared up at the boy defiantly, refusing to answer. She was turning out to be a tough little cookie, Baylor thought—a lot tougher than she looked.

Milo peered into the backpack, pulled out her brown sweater and tossed it aside, then extracted a pair of underwear—sensible white cotton briefs. He made a clicking noise with his tongue. "Not very imaginative, chicky. Doesn't that big, handsome cop boyfriend of yours have anything to say about this?"

It took every ounce of Baylor's willpower to keep his mouth shut. He wanted to pulverize that little scumbag. Every muscle in his body tensed, coiled to spring into action. All he needed was the right moment.

"He's not my boyfriend," Camille said in a small voice.

The next thing to come out of the pack was a little white box. Baylor held his breath as Milo pulled off his dark glasses and opened the box, examining the contents. Even from several feet away, Baylor could guess what was in there. Computer diskettes, damn it. Any last shred of hope he'd held for Camille's innocence melted away.

"What's this?" Milo asked.

"It's nothing important," Camille answered too quickly, too brightly. Her lie wasn't very convincing.

Milo narrowed his eyes into slits. "Nothing important, huh? How about I just toss the box into the water?" He took two quick strides toward the bay door before Camille cried out.

"No, wait! Don't destroy my diskettes, please." Then, in a stronger voice, "If you want that reward I mentioned, you'll let me have them back."

Milo folded his arms, letting the box dangle from his fingertips. "How much did you say you'd pay me?"

"Five hundred dollars," she answered.

"And how do you propose to come up with the money?"

"I've got it right here, in traveler's checks. I can sign them over to you, and you can take them to any bank—"

"I don't do business with banks," Milo interrupted, though he sauntered to the wallet he'd discarded minutes earlier and flipped through the checks with renewed interest. A nasty smile formed on his thin lips. "For your information, lady, I can take these checks and convert them to cash, with or without you signing them, just like that." He snapped his fingers. "The Dawgs have connections."

Camille's face clouded with anger. "You do that and I'll have you arrested. Don't be stupid. I offered a more-than-generous reward. There's no reason—" But her words were cut off as Milo dropped to his knees in front of her, his big knife pointed right at her throat.

"No one calls me stupid, chicky," he said. "Apologize."

That was more than Baylor needed to see. In one swift movement he slammed the bay door open and burst into the warehouse, his gun aimed straight at Milo's back. "Freeze, you little creep!"

The other three teenagers reflexively thrust their hands into the air. Baylor expected Milo to do the same. But instead the kid whipped around with the speed of light; all at once he was crouching behind Camille, his knife at her throat.

"Let her go," Baylor demanded, his voice thundering through the empty warehouse.

"Drop the gun," Milo countered, hauling Camille to her feet, "or I'll cut your girlfriend here."

Baylor paled at the thought of that sharp blade marring Camille's fragile beauty. Still, he forced himself to smile, as if he had everything under control. "She's not my girlfriend, and come to think of it you can do whatever you like with her. All I want is that box.'' He nodded toward the computer diskettes Milo had dropped.

The boy and the man stared at each other for several silent heartbeats, sizing each other up as a biting wind whipped through the warehouse from the open bay door. Baylor felt vulnerable so close to the opening. If Milo rushed him he could fall right over the edge. He inched away from the door, but as he did Milo moved closer to it, Camille in tow. Baylor froze, alert to the new danger.

''So, you don't care about the little chicky here, huh?'' Baylor didn't answer.

''Which would you rather save, the girl or the box? Take your pick.'' With that he gave Camille a shove toward the door, pushing her just hard enough that she teetered on the edge of the warehouse flooring. One misstep, one errant gust of wind, and she would plummet to the cold waters of the bay below.

The choice was no contest for Baylor. He lunged for Camille just as Milo gave her one final nudge. Baylor grasped her around the waist with one arm while the other flailed madly to keep his balance, but his efforts weren't enough; he felt them both toppling over the edge, as if in slow motion.

He made one final, desperate attempt to save them, dropping his gun and reaching out with his free arm toward a rope that dangled from the ancient pulley. Amazingly, his hand closed around the fat piece of hemp. *This is crazy,* he thought as his arm jerked practically out of its socket and the rope fibers burned his palm. *How did Tarzan make it look so easy?*

For a few breathless moments they were suspended above the water while Baylor's muscles and tendons screamed in protest at the abuse. But the combined weight of two people was too much for the rotting rope. Even as Baylor swung his legs wildly, trying to make contact with the pulley framework, he could feel the rope's fibers stretching and breaking one by one.

"I can't swim!" Camille cried out as their last connection to anything solid gave way with an audible ping. Then the wind was rushing past them and the cold, black water reached up to swallow them.

Chapter Five

Camille clenched her eyes shut, as if that might halt the rocketing, headlong fall. She started to scream, but the sound was cut short by the water's shocking impact.

A cold blackness engulfed her. It swirled under her clothes and through her hair, into her nose and mouth and ears, obliterating light and sound, plunging her into a tomb of nonsensations. She wanted to struggle against the numbing force of the water, to drag herself up to the surface, but "up" could have been any direction. Gravity had ceased to exist. Her fear of sinking deeper was so powerful that it paralyzed her. She held herself still and rigid, eyes tightly shut, and waited....

It was only when something grabbed her by the hair and yanked that she began to struggle. The water had hands, and it was trying to hold her under. She thrashed with every ounce of energy she could muster, kicking with leaden feet and jabbing with her elbows, though every movement was hampered by a strange lethargy. Technicolor spots danced behind her eyelids. Her chest felt as if it might explode.

Abruptly she broke the water's surface. She tried to breathe but succeeded only in choking. The hands were dragging on her again. She fought against them.

"Dammit, Camille, stop struggling or you'll drown us both."

Baylor! That was Baylor's voice. She tried to call to him for help but couldn't get any words past her constricted throat. She clawed at the arm that had clamped around her neck. It loosened its hold for an instant. She struggled free and slipped under the relentless water.

Once again she was hauled above the surface. The wind felt like liquid ice as it blew against her wet skin and hair. By comparison the water was comfortable. Suddenly it seemed imperative that she reclaim her warm water blanket, and she fought like a demon to do so.

"Be *still*!" Something hard struck her face. There was no pain, just an explosion of pretty stars behind her eyelids. She reached one hand out, thinking she could touch the stars, but before she could they faded into black. . . .

When she awoke, Camille was face down on cold concrete, and something heavy was pushing hard against her back, then bending her elbows behind her head with painful jerks. She heard someone coughing and gasping. She realized it was herself.

As oxygen worked its way into her lungs and then her brain, she became gradually aware of several uncomfortable sensations. Her chest burned as though it was on fire, and the side of her face throbbed with pain. And if that clod on her back stretched her elbows behind her head one more time—

"Ouch! Stop it," she protested.

"Thank God." The hands, no longer threatening, pulled
her off the pavement and hauled her against a soggy
sweatshirt, then proceeded to squeeze her in an overen-
thusiastic hug until she was sure her bones would break.
"Thank God," he said again. "I thought you'd drowned."

"Let me go," she commanded in a croaky voice.

"It's all right, you're safe now." Baylor stroked her wet,
tangled hair, most of which had pulled free of its elastic
band. He rocked her gently back and forth, despite her
feeble struggles.

"Safe from whom?" she muttered.

He stopped rocking and pulled her chin up until she was
forced to look at him. His eyes narrowed, just slightly.
"You would have drowned if I hadn't dragged you to
shore."

"And I never would have fallen in the water in the first
place if you hadn't blundered onto the scene and then
knocked me over the edge," she pointed out. "If you saved
me from drowning, it must have been an accident. You
don't care what happens to me. You even said so, to Milo."

"Did it occur to you I might have been lying?" he asked
softly. "I was trying to divert Milo's attention away from
you."

She opened her mouth to hurl another accusation, but
the words never formed. As the scene they'd played out
with the Dawgs rushed to the forefront of her memory with
crystal-clear horror, she suddenly lost the urge to argue.
She could have died up in that warehouse. She shuddered
to think what would have happened to her if Baylor hadn't
arrived.

"I'm s-sorry," she said with a small shudder. "I don't
know why I attacked you like that. You s-saved my l-life."
Her teeth chattered with the cold.

"You made it damned difficult, too," said Baylor, but there was no longer any censure in his voice. "How do you feel? Think you can walk to the car?"

She tried but couldn't. Her legs, still numb with cold, supported her about as well as two strips of raw bacon. Baylor scooped her into his arms and carried her, seemingly without effort. She clung to him shamelessly as she relived the terror of Milo's taunts and threats, and the smothering black water. Her whole body shook in delayed reaction to the trauma.

He set her gently into the passenger seat of his old sedan. She protested weakly when he pulled away from her, so he smoothed a damp strand of hair off her face with murmured words of comfort. "I'll be right back." He pressed his lips against her forehead in a strangely sensuous gesture before closing the door.

It felt better just to be out of the wind. Camille wrapped her arms around herself and shivered. She'd never been this physically uncomfortable, never. Yet she felt strangely elated, too. The very fact that she felt the stinging cold was an indication that she was alive, and at the moment that seemed wondrous.

When Baylor reappeared, climbing into the driver's seat, he tossed a rough wool blanket to Camille. "I found this in the trunk. Dry yourself off," he said as he started the engine and adjusted the heater controls.

When the blanket had absorbed some of the excess moisture from her skin and clothing, she handed it back to Baylor. He ran it quickly over his face and hair, then immediately returned it to Camille, solicitously wrapping it around her trembling shoulders. Soon the hot air from the heater was filling the car, radiating through the blanket and surrounding her in a comforting cocoon of warmth.

As the cold receded, so did the tremors of fear. With Baylor just an arm's length away she felt safe and protected. A million unanswered questions stood between them, yet for some reason she trusted him, for the moment at least. Time enough later to ask questions.

"Feeling better?" he asked after a while.

"Much."

He studied her face, as if to ascertain whether she was telling the truth. "I think I should take you to a hospital," he said, brushing his fingertips lightly along her bruised cheek. "You took a pretty nasty wallop."

His light touch gave her a shiver of awareness. She reached up with her own hand to retrace the path of his fingers. "How did that happen?" she asked, puzzled. "I know I hit the water with a smack, but..."

He averted his eyes, his guilty flush unmistakable.

"*You* did this to me?"

"You were fighting me like a wildcat. I had to do something or you would have dragged both of us under the water. I only intended to bring you to your senses, but I, uh..."

"Knocked me unconscious," she finished for him, but it wasn't an accusation. "You probably did the right thing."

"I don't know about that." Again he stroked her face, his touch as light as a rose petal. "Does it hurt? Are you hurt anywhere else?"

"Not seriously. But now that the numbness is going away I ache all over." She looked down at herself, just to make sure she wasn't bleeding. She knew that endorphins in the bloodstream could prevent accident victims from feeling the pain of their injuries. But both legs and both arms appeared intact.

She also noticed that her wet sweater clung to her breasts with uncompromising thoroughness. Reflexively she pulled the blanket closer, but not soon enough, judging from the sudden fiery sparkle in Baylor's eyes.

She cleared her throat. "I don't think a hospital is necessary. I'll be fine." As she said this she realized she was more than fine. She was downright healthy, if physiology was any indicator. Her nipples had risen into hard peaks in response to Baylor's intimate gaze, and she could easily imagine his hands roaming where his eyes had. "At least, everything seems to be functioning," she added, feeling a warm blush creep into her face.

"But you might have a concussion," he said as he continued to study her, doubt clouding his expression. "Damn, I can't believe I hit you. I've never hit a woman before."

"It doesn't hurt much," she lied, breaking eye contact, leaning away from him to lessen the growing intimacy. Ten minutes ago she'd almost died. Physical desire toward her rescuer must be some sort of syndrome, she imagined—a response to excess adrenaline or something. To distract herself she stretched up so she could examine her face in the rearview mirror. When she did she wished she hadn't. She looked like she'd had a losing confrontation with an eighteen wheeler.

"You're going to have quite a shiner," he said. "I really think a doctor—"

"My vision is clear and I'm not dizzy," she interrupted. "A hot bath and some chicken soup is all the medicine I need."

He paused before speaking, as if weighing the wisdom of her choice. "If you're sure," he finally said. "But I intend to keep an eye on you." He slid away from her with seeming reluctance, to settle himself into the driver's seat.

"You've *been* keeping an eye on me," she said as he put the car in gear. "It's not that I'm not grateful, mind you, but I'd like to know why."

He gave her a sideways glance. "You have to ask? The computer diskettes were right there, in plain sight."

"Yes, but what about them?"

"What about them?" he repeated incredulously. "I believe you offered five hundred dollars for their return. You'd have gotten quite a bargain."

"I would have?" She started to ask Baylor what he was talking about when she realized he'd stopped the car in front of the warehouse. "You're not going back in there, are you?"

"Don't worry, the Dawgs are long gone. I just want to see if they left anything behind. How did you get in?"

"There's a loose board on a window, toward the back on the right side."

"Okay," he said, opening his door. "I'll be back in—" He paused.

"What's wrong?"

He leaned toward her and opened the glove compartment, then extracted a narrow strip of white plastic. "Sorry, Camille. I know this isn't fair, after all you've just been through, but I can't take any more chances." Before she could blink he'd fastened her wrist to the door handle with the plastic device.

"Hey, you can't do this!" she protested, but he was already gone, loping around the corner of the warehouse. *Of all the nerve!* She'd have him arrested, that's what she'd do. Surely it wasn't legal for him to handcuff her when he was no longer on the police force.

She fumed and muttered to herself until he returned, a long two minutes later. He had her shopping bags and backpack with him. She should have been elated, but she was too furious to rejoice in the return of her things.

Baylor opened the back door and thrust the bags inside the car. "They took the disks, but they ran off in such a hurry that they left everything else behind. Even your traveler's checks," he added with a victorious grin.

"Take this handcuff thing off me right now, Baylor Pierce," she warned in what she hoped was a menacing voice, "or you will be extremely sorry. Whatever Paul hired you to do, he would not condone your manhandling me."

The grin vanished. "All right, take it easy." He produced a pocket knife and cut her free. "I hate to break it to you, but Paul would like nothing better than to see you in jail."

"Jail?" Camille squeaked. That gave her pause. Could she go to jail for breaking her employment contract with Easterwood? Or had she done something else wrong? She remained silent, pondering the possibilities, until they'd arrived back in Baylor's neighborhood. "What exactly is it I'm supposed to be guilty of?" she asked cautiously as he circled the block, looking for a place to park.

"You can stop playing games. I know all about M23."

This was getting more and more strange. "Obviously you know something about M23 that eludes me," she said. "Why don't you fill me in."

"Are you going to deny you stole the M23 data?"

"*Stole* it?" she shrieked. "*Me?* How could you possibly believe such a thing?"

Baylor shrugged. "It disappeared from Easterwood about the same time you did. I'll admit, I had a hard time believing you were a thief. I mean, you don't exactly fit the mold. But—"

Camille interrupted. "You mean Project M23 disappeared? The whole thing? Oh, my Lord, this is terrible, disastrous! That project represents years of intense work, Paul's and mine." She paused, then turned her suddenly fierce hazel eyes on Baylor. "How dare you accuse me of stealing something without a shred of evidence—"

"Whoa, hold on there. I have evidence." This was hardly the reaction Baylor had expected. How did Camille have the nerve to play innocent when she *knew* he'd seen the disks? "If you didn't steal it, then what's on those computer disks you wanted to pay five hundred dollars for?"

"You mean you thought—"

"Just answer the question, Camille. What's on the disks?"

"You're going to feel very silly when I tell you."

"Try me."

She sighed. "The disks contain personal notes, kind of like a diary. I've been jotting things down on my computer for years, always thinking in the back of my mind that I'd turn the notes into a book someday."

"What kind of book?" he asked, forgetting for the moment that he didn't believe her.

She answered his question with another question. "How much do you know about my background?"

"Not that much. I read your personnel file at Easterwood. Paul filled in a few of the details."

"Then you know I'm not . . . average."

Not by any stretch of the imagination, he thought as he darted into a parking place. He didn't respond aloud, however, until they were safely inside his apartment. "I know you're exceptionally intelligent and extremely well educated," he said, cranking up the furnace. " 'Gifted,' I guess they call that now."

"In many ways I am gifted," she acknowledged, sinking gingerly onto the edge of his couch. "But do you have any idea what it's like to be a child trying to cope with that gift? I was miserable most of the time, and it shouldn't have been that way. Looking back, I wish I'd handled things differently."

Baylor had to admit he was intrigued. "And that's the book you want to write?" he asked, sitting across from her. "Your experiences?"

"More like a self-help book for gifted children. I'd like to think I could prevent some kids from making the same mistakes I did. Anyway, that's what's on the disks that the Dawgs stole—notes for my book."

Baylor was silent for a long time. If she was telling a lie, it was a damn convincing one. She looked so young, so vulnerable. How could he possibly accuse her of a crime? "Why don't you get out of those wet clothes," he said. "Take a long, hot bath, and I'll rustle up that chicken soup you mentioned."

She stared at him for a moment, her lower lip barely trembling. "You don't believe me, do you?"

"I'm not sure what to believe."

At that she closed herself off. Her expression became uncharacteristically hard and impassive as she rose from the couch. "I'll take that bath. But I'll pass on the soup. You and Paul and the Dawgs can have your silly cloak-and-dagger games. I'm getting out of here."

"Suppose I don't want you to leave."

"How are you going to stop me, handcuff me again? I don't think you're dumb enough to actually kidnap me. If you are, *you'll* be the one going to jail." With that she flounced toward the bathroom, her shopping bags in tow.

She was right, he thought as he emptied a can of chicken noodle into a saucepan. In a few minutes she was going to walk out of here, and there wasn't a damn thing he could do about it short of physically restraining her. And that was out of the question.

As to whether he believed her story...he'd watched and listened as she'd tried to lie to Milo, and she'd done a lousy job. Yet just now she'd sounded sincere even to his jaded ears. Normally Baylor had a sixth sense when it came to people lying. Every instinct told him Camille Gordon was telling the truth.

Still, he had to keep reminding himself that his instinct had proven itself less than reliable. And with all the evidence piled up against her...after all, what were the chances that she'd just *happen* to be carrying a box of disks that had nothing to do with M23?

He found some leftover fried chicken in the refrigerator, so he removed the skin, cut up the meat and added it to the pot. While he waited for the soup to heat, he called his captain to report the lost gun. The explanation got a bit sticky, given that Baylor wasn't supposed to be using the gun, but thankfully the old man didn't press for too many details.

After that chore was accomplished, Baylor called Paul again. "I found her," he said.

"And?"

"The disks are still at large."

Paul muttered something disagreeable under his breath.

"Listen, Paul, in a few minutes Camille will be walking out of my apartment, and I'm going to let her go. If you want to follow her, fine. Personally I...I'm not so sure she's guilty."

"Well I am—there's no doubt, Baylor, none. Look at the evidence!"

"Maybe someone set her up."

"Oh, come off it. Why don't you admit you're falling for that innocent act of hers."

Baylor thought about this for a moment. "Maybe." And maybe he was just plain falling for her. He couldn't deny a physical attraction, not after the way his body had reacted to the sight of her in that clinging sweater. "Anyway," he continued, "even if she did steal that data, I don't think she'll go after the disks again, not after what happened this morning."

"All right, I'm game. What happened this morning?"

"We tangled with the Dawgs and almost got ourselves killed," Baylor stated matter-of-factly. "She's good and scared now, and frankly so am I. My advice is to hire a P.I. to go after the Dawgs. I don't think you need to worry about Camille any longer."

"What about the package she mailed?" said Paul. "She'll try to reclaim that sooner or later."

The package. Baylor had forgotten about that. "I'll see what I can find out," he agreed with a hopeless sigh. "But then I'm finished with this case. Do I make myself clear?"

"Perfectly. Maybe I should call the police after all and have Camille arrested."

Baylor's heart skipped erratically as a series of images danced in his mind, images of Camille being taken away by gruff, uniformed patrolmen, then sitting in a holding cell with prostitutes and drug addicts. She'd have no one to call for help, no family or friends to find her a good lawyer.... "Don't get the police involved," he said quietly, knowing full well he was succumbing to Paul's manipulations. Paul was good at that. "I'll follow her."

"I'll wait by the phone." There was a note of triumph in Paul's voice.

Baylor grumbled to himself as he poured some of the soup into a bowl. Between Paul and Camille, he'd somehow lost control of his life.

He caught her scent before he heard her behind him. She smelled of his soap and his shampoo, but somehow on her they were different. Softer. Sexier.

"You made the soup, anyway." Her tone was surprisingly conciliatory.

"I figured you might change your mind," he said without turning around to look at her. "Go sit down and I'll bring you a bowl."

"Are you sure you don't mind feeding a thief and a liar?" The question was laced with challenge.

He turned quickly to face her, sloshing a bit of the soup onto the floor. "What would you say if I told you I believe your story?"

"I'd say *you're* the liar," she said, taking the bowl from him and walking slowly toward the dining area. "You've got skepticism written all over your face."

He studied her from behind, nodding approval at the pale pink sweatshirt, festooned with a pattern of shiny beads, and the matching pink denim jeans that molded themselves to her very shapely posterior. Her hair descended in damp chestnut waves over her shoulders and halfway down her back.

She settled herself in a chair, then took an experimental sip of broth. "Mmm, that hits the spot. Aren't you going to have some?"

"I thought I'd wash Boston Harbor off me before I joined you. But if I leave to take a shower—"

"I'm not going to run away again," she said, reading his thoughts. "I changed my mind. I thought about this whole thing while I took my bath, and I decided that if I've been accused of stealing something, I ought to stick around long enough to clear myself.''

''And how do you propose to do that?'' Baylor asked.

''We're going to get those computer disks back, of course, if for no other reason than to prove to you that I'm telling the truth.''

''We? You mean, you and me, together?''

''Exactly. I figure we'd be a lot more successful if we'd combine our resources.''

''Your brains and my brawn?'' Baylor suggested, bristling. Just because she'd outfoxed him a couple of times—

''My logic and your street smarts,'' she corrected him gently. ''I had no trouble locating the stolen backpack, but I was definitely out of my element in dealing with the Dawgs. You, on the other hand—''

''Yeah, I get the picture.'' He had to admit she was making sense.

''So what do you say?''

He didn't have to think long. ''You're on, Smart Stuff. You got yourself a partner.'' The idea appealed to him for more reasons than one.

Chapter Six

"So what do you see as our first official action as partners?" Baylor asked as he settled at one end of the sofa in his living room. Camille sat at the other end, holding an ice pack to her face, her bare feet tucked under her. She'd been perusing his magazine collection while he showered. The pages of a men's periodical had yielded quite an education.

"I think we should pay a visit to In-Ho Nguyen's home," she answered without hesitation, having already decided their next move. "Is this really your feminine ideal?" She held up the magazine centerfold, which featured a curvaceous blonde wearing a hard hat and a tool belt—and nothing else. "I had no idea—"

Baylor snatched the magazine out of Camille's hand and dropped it face down on the coffee table. "I buy it for the articles. Can we please get back to business?"

She suppressed a smile. Baylor's gruffness didn't fool her. He was embarrassed, just as he'd been when he'd ad-

mitted to hitting her in the face. For some reason she found
the quality charming in such a big, all-male man. "Business it is," she replied cheerfully. "I figure In-Ho is the
victim of tremendous peer pressure, as any gang member
might be. He's more likely to cooperate with us if we can
talk to him alone, away from that awful Milo."

Baylor nodded in agreement. "I'll call my former partner and try to get an address." He started to rise.

"Three-twenty-eight Pearl Street, Apartment F," Camille said, rattling off In-Ho's address from memory.

Baylor sank back onto the sofa and stared at her. "And
how, pray tell, do you know that? For your information,
it's a felony to hack your way into the police computer."

She smiled enigmatically. "Why should that concern
me?"

"I suppose you pulled that address out of the air?"

"An acquaintance provided me with the information on
the Dawgs," she explained, turning serious. "I can't tell
you who it is or I'd be violating a confidence."

He seemed to consider this as he absently massaged his
right shoulder.

"Is something wrong with your arm?" she asked with
sudden concern. She'd been so caught up in her own
physical miseries, it hadn't even occurred to her that Baylor might have injured himself during their ordeal.

"Nothing's wrong," he said, folding his arms in an instinctively protective gesture. But not before Camille
caught a glimpse of the angry red blisters on the palm of
his hand.

She inhaled sharply. "You *are* hurt," she said, sliding
closer to him and taking hold of his arm. "Let me see."

Reluctantly he showed her his abrasions.

"How did that happen?" she asked, trying to ignore the inappropriate pleasure she derived from letting his big, capable hand rest in her much smaller one.

"Rope burn. That's what I get for acting like a comic-book hero. Rope burn and a host of strained muscles."

"You should put something on those blisters," she said, feeling suddenly protective of him. "No telling what sort of nasty germs you picked up from that rope, not to mention the filth in Boston Harbor."

"That's not necessary—" he started to say, but she shushed him.

The nurturing instinct was a pleasant but unfamiliar one, she thought as she went to get some first-aid cream from her backpack. She'd never had to worry about anyone else before. Not that the man needed nurturing, she mused, reaching into a zipper compartment of her pack for the tube of ointment. He was about the most self-sufficient person she could imagine.

She squirted a generous amount of the cream into Baylor's hand despite his protests. After an initial struggle, he allowed her to minister to him, though she could tell he was a bundle of tension. "This doesn't hurt, does it?" she asked, soothing the cream into his skin with light, languid strokes.

"No," he answered in a strangely breathless voice.

"Do you have any gauze?" She kept hold of his hand far longer than necessary. She just couldn't seem to let go of him.

"No," he said again. "I wouldn't want my hand bandaged, anyway. It might prove to be a handicap."

"You're not planning to climb up the sides of any more buildings, are you? Or use your gun?"

"Not if I can help it. Anyway, my gun is at the bottom of the harbor." He extracted his hand from her solicitous grip.

Somehow she managed to back away from him and return to the end of the couch where she belonged. "Before we go to see In-Ho, would you tell me the whole story? How M23 disappeared and why you and Paul think I stole it? I'd like to know exactly how and why you're involved, too."

He sighed. "All right. I suppose you deserve some explanation."

Camille listened intently as Baylor told her how Paul had asked him to find her, and the subsequent discovery that M23's data files were missing. She hoped to key in on some detail Baylor had missed, something that would provide a clue as to who was the actual thief. But the facts left her mystified.

"Then there was that big package you mailed the day you left Easterwood," he said, "just the right size for the missing physical components."

She gave him a blank look, but slowly a memory asserted itself. "There was a package sitting by the department 'out' basket," she said, closing her eyes and trying to remember. "I had to pass the mail room on my way to the dentist anyway, so I took the package with me. I do that all the time. We all do—Paul, Nita, everybody."

"And you don't know what was in it?"

"No."

Baylor scowled. "I'd give anything to know who it went to."

"Oh, I can tell you that," Camille said matter-of-factly. "It was addressed to a J. Cordaro at a post office box in Somerville. I can't remember the exact number, but it had three digits. Nine-seven . . . something."

"You mean to tell me you remember all that just from glancing at the address when you dropped it off at the mail room?"

She nodded. "It's a handy little talent, sometimes."

"What about that voice mail message you left for Paul?"

She shrugged. "What about it?"

"It sounded like a confession to me."

Again she was confused. "I apologized to Paul for not being able to stay and finish my work on the Project. And I reassured him that the work could go on, with or without my input, and I wished him success with it. How could you construe that as a confession?"

Baylor shook his head. "That's not what you said on the message I listened to. You announced that you had to leave Easterwood, and then you said, 'Sorry about M23.' That was it."

She raised an indignant eyebrow. "Obviously the message you heard is not the one I left."

"Could someone have tampered with it?" he asked. "Is that possible?"

She nodded thoughtfully, relieved to at least consider the possibility that someone else was the culprit. "I suppose someone could have erased my message and recorded a different one, imitating my voice..."

Baylor shook his head. "It was your voice. I'm sure. I have a good ear for that kind of thing."

"All right then, someone could have simply erased the last half of the message, leaving only the part you heard. Or they could have spliced in words. But..."

"But what?"

"The voice mail system is very secure. You'd have to know Paul's access code to even hear the message, and to alter the tape—I just can't imagine how it would be done."

"There's hardly a security system in existence that can't be breached. Not even the police department's," he added pointedly as he stood. "Come on, let's get going. We can talk more about this later on."

It wasn't a long drive to Boston's small, colorful Chinatown. Since the drizzle had stopped and the sun was peeking through the clouds, the street was crowded with midday traffic of every description. Taxis full of tourists cruised for bargains in jade or porcelain; young people on delivery bikes raced along their routes to their next destination; and pedestrians jammed the sidewalks to peruse the wares at fruit and vegetable stalls, newsstands and fish markets.

Camille opened her window and inhaled deeply of the air scented with myriad fragrances—leather, spices, perfumes. "What a place!" she exclaimed. She'd had no idea such an exotic setting existed so close to home. She had never come near Chinatown during her short, infrequent forays into the real world.

Baylor only smiled indulgently at her enthusiasm. She must appear very childish, she realized, getting so excited over something that was obviously commonplace to him. But that didn't dampen her high spirits in the least. This was life, and she wanted to see all of it.

In-Ho's apartment building, an ugly pile of brown bricks Camille could only describe as a tenement, sat on a narrow, less-than-glamorous Chinatown back street. Parking was impossible, so they settled for a public garage several blocks away, which charged an exorbitant fee.

"Nervous?" Baylor asked as they approached the front door.

She realized she had been clutching the sleeve of his jacket. "A little. I'm not used to crowds."

"I hope you'll let me do the talking," he said as he opened the door and allowed her to pass through it ahead of him into the dingy foyer.

"I won't say a word," Camille readily agreed. "My job is to locate the disks. You can do the people work."

They wound their way to the second floor on a narrow staircase, its green carpet worn slick by years of foot-traffic. Exotic cooking odors came from somewhere. Camille found them not unpleasant. "Let's have Chinese food for dinner," she said as they searched for the door marked F. "I'll buy."

Baylor made no response to her frivolous suggestion as he located the correct apartment. He took a deep breath and rapped sharply on the door.

After a long pause, they heard the scrape of a dead bolt. The door opened a crack, still fastened with a chain, and half of a woman's face could be seen peeking through the opening. She said something in a language Camille didn't understand.

"Do you speak English?" Baylor asked slowly.

She nodded. "What do you want?"

"We're looking for In-Ho Nguyen. Does he live here?" Baylor stepped back so she could see Camille.

The woman's one visible eye widened in surprise, or perhaps fear. "You police?"

"No," Baylor answered.

"My brother has done something wrong?"

"Yes." Baylor put his hand against the door to prevent the woman from closing it. "But we just want to talk to him," he clarified. "We don't want him to get in trouble."

With seeming reluctance, she opened the door and admitted them to the apartment. It was small and sparsely furnished, Camille noted, but it also was scrupulously clean. The woman herself was tiny—even smaller than Camille—with thick, black hair caught in a ponytail, and she wore a neat cotton dress. Through an open door Camille caught a glimpse of an old woman working at a sewing machine, oblivious to the visitors.

"Sit down," In-Ho's sister said with grudging cordiality. "I will get tea."

Camille was anxious to get on with their business, but Baylor cautioned her with his eyes not to be too impatient. To turn down the tea might be an insult, she figured, so she kept quiet as she'd promised. The young Asian woman returned shortly with cups containing a green-colored brew. Camille added lots of sugar and hoped for the best.

With a short, stiff bow, In-Ho's sister told them her name was Kim-Li. Baylor returned the introduction, then proceeded to explain the events surrounding Camille's stolen backpack. He gave the story an air of lightness by smiling often, seeming to treat In-Ho's crime as a mild offense. "We don't want to involve the police," he said at last. "We simply want the white box returned, and we're willing to offer a reward. Five hundred dollars."

Kim-Li paled. "So much money? This box is valuable, then?"

"Valuable only to me," Camille inserted, forgetting her promise to keep quiet.

Kim-Li shook her head. "In-Ho is not here. On Mondays and Wednesdays he works for the city, so he doesn't have to go back to detention."

"The job is part of his parole?" Baylor asked.

"Yes, that's right. Parole."

"When do you expect him back?"

She shrugged her narrow shoulders uncomfortably. "I do not know. He stays out late with those terrible boys, even though his parole officer says he should not. Sometimes he does not come home for many days." She seemed close to tears. "My husband and I work very hard to bring my family here, so In-Ho can go to school and get a good job, and maybe become rich. And what does he do? He skips school, steals cars...."

"Can we leave a note for him?" Baylor asked, declining to offer any comforting words. There wasn't much comfort to offer.

Kim-Li recovered quickly. "Yes, that would be well." She went to get paper and pencil.

"It's sad, isn't it?" Camille whispered.

Baylor nodded. "Sometimes kids rebel against their families in strange ways. I ought to know."

Me, too, she mused, thinking of her own recent rebellion. It had taken her twenty-five years to figure out that she didn't really want the life her father had mapped out for her. She'd finally rebelled by running away from it. She wondered what exactly Baylor knew of rebellion, but there was no time to ask just now. Kim-Li was returning with a pad of paper and a pen.

Baylor printed the note carefully, using his own name and phone number. Underneath he wrote, "$500 cash for return of disks, no questions asked."

"If you want to look for him, go to the Common," Kim-Li added as they were leaving. "That is where he works, picking up trash."

"Thank you," they said together as she closed the door behind them.

"Do you think he'll call?" Camille asked when they were once again outside and walking at a brisk pace toward the parking garage.

"I think we'll get some response. It's hard for a kid to turn down an easy five hundred bucks. But we might have to wait awhile."

"We could go to the Common and look for him," she said when they were inside the car.

"Maybe later. Right now I think we should pay a visit to the Somerville Post Office. Can you act?"

"Act like what?"

"Like Mrs. J. Cordaro. Pretend you're Mrs. Cordaro and you're expecting an important package, and ask them to double-check and see if it's arrived."

"Why can't you do it?" she objected.

"Because the postal workers might be more open to you than me. You look more innocent."

"But I'm not a good liar."

Baylor sighed. "I wish I could believe that."

"You still think I did it, don't you?" It hurt. His lack of trust was a spear that stabbed all the way to her heart. Now that they were working together, she'd begun to hope that Baylor was starting to believe in her. Obviously she'd been wrong. The opinion of one ex-policeman shouldn't have mattered so much. But it did.

"I want to believe you, really," he said after he'd paid the parking garage attendant. "But I don't want to be a sucker, either, just because you seem...nice. Ten years on the police force taught me that criminals come in all shapes, sizes and sexes."

"But why would I want to steal M23?" she asked, fighting despair.

"Money. Revenge. Any number of reasons. Look, I could have taken you straight to Paul last night and washed my hands of this whole thing. Instead I'm giving you the benefit of a doubt, despite what Paul thinks. It's the best I can do."

For now she'd have to settle for that, she decided, though she had to fight a bitter taste in her mouth. No one had ever doubted her word before. Until today she'd never been accused of even the smallest transgression.

After a bit of coaching, she did an adequate job posing as Mrs. Cordaro, inquiring about the package in a shaking voice while Baylor bought stamps at the next window. The results were disappointing. The postal worker informed her that Box 973 had been cleaned out and closed just that morning.

"Could you hear?" she asked Baylor as they left the Somerville Post Office.

"I heard. Closed just this morning, huh? The package must have arrived safely, then. By the way, where were *you* this morning?"

"I was sitting in a bakery waiting for a phone call," she answered huffily, slamming the car door with more-than-necessary vigor. "It's four or five blocks from your house. I sat there for at least two hours, and the cashier will remember me. She kept staring at me, wondering why I didn't leave."

"And what's the name of this bakery?" he asked good-naturedly.

"It's the . . . um . . ."

"Yes, Miss Perfect Recall?"

She closed her eyes, trying to force the memory of the bakery's front door into focus. But after a minute or so she had to admit defeat. "I can't remember. I must not have paid attention."

"Uh-huh." He looked faintly amused.

She groaned. "You don't believe me. Again."

"You have to admit it looks pretty suspicious, your just happening to forget the name of the place that could provide you with an alibi for picking up that package."

"I remember exactly where it is. Drive back to your neighborhood and I'll show you," she challenged.

"You can show me later," he replied, apparently unconcerned with her alibi. "Let's go back to the Common. Maybe we can catch up with In-Ho."

Camille agreed, though she was already growing weary of this chase. She was glad she hadn't chosen police work as a career.

They parked near a T stop, then took the subway to the Park Street station. From there they rode a creaky wooden escalator up to street level and found themselves right in the heart of the Boston Common. Camille was still amazed at how efficiently the underground train could move her from one place to another, though the crowds made her edgy.

She and Baylor both scanned the Common for any sign of their quarry, but In-Ho was nowhere to be seen.

"It's a big park," Camille said. "Maybe we should split up. We could cover more ground—"

"Not a chance." Baylor grabbed on to her hand with a steely grip. "Let's try this way first."

She had no choice but to follow. "You don't actually think I'd run away again, do you? I told you I wouldn't."

"I was thinking more of your safety. I won't have you confronting that juvenile thug alone."

"Oh." His protective tone gave her a warm, fuzzy feeling. She quickened her pace so she could keep up with him. After a few minutes his grip on her loosened, until they were merely holding hands like any two lovers on a leisurely walk through the park.

Instead of searching for In-Ho, her eyes wandered to the strong, serious man beside her. His blue plaid flannel shirt stretched tautly over wide shoulders, the sleeves rolled up to reveal firmly muscled forearms. In the bright spring sun his eyes were a vivid green.

Lord, he was handsome. It was surprisingly easy to imagine that he *was* her lover, she mused, letting an evocative daydream run its course. Only when he glanced down at her and caught her staring did she snap herself back into the present.

They circled the park, then crisscrossed it, but by the time they'd returned to their starting point, they'd seen no sign of In-Ho.

"It was worth a try," Baylor said with a shrug. He was still thinking about that hungry look he'd seen in Camille's eyes and wondered what it meant. "I suppose there's nothing left to do except go home and wait by the phone."

They turned toward the subway entrance, but after a few steps, Camille stopped, looking down at her feet. "What's this red line on the pavement?"

"That's the Freedom Trail. Don't tell me you've never walked it."

"I don't even know what it is."

"You follow the red line, and it leads you past all the historical sites connected with the Revolution—the Old North Church, Paul Revere's house. How could you live in Boston your whole life and not do the Freedom Trail?"

She shrugged. "I didn't get out much. Can we do it? After all, we don't have any other pressing engagements."

He consulted his watch. "Sure, why not." It was almost three, but they could take in a few of the sights before dark. Even if they rushed home to wait by the phone, it wasn't likely that In-Ho would call them so soon.

Baylor allowed himself to relax for the first time in two days as he followed Camille along the red line to their first stop, the State House on Beacon Hill. He hadn't walked the Freedom Trail in years. It might be fun, seeing everything through her fresh eyes.

She studied the gold-domed structure with quiet concentration and read every word on the commemorative plaque but said nothing. They moved on to their next stop, the graceful Park Street Church. Again she studied the architecture and read the plaque, still offering no comment. Baylor was beginning to wonder if she was enjoying herself at all when they reached the Old Granary Burying Ground. There her enthusiasm suddenly bubbled to the surface.

"I can't believe how old these graves are!" she exclaimed, dropping to her knees to study one of the more ornate headstones. "Look, this woman died more than three hundred years ago. And she was only twenty-four—that's younger than I am." She ran her hand reverently over the faded etchings in the stone. "I've never touched anything this old before," she said softly. "My whole life, everything I dealt with was new—the newest technology, the most recently published books available. I never thought . . . this is silly, but I never thought an old headstone could be so thrilling."

She stood quickly and moved on to study a monument. "Look, Baylor, the victims of the Boston Massacre."

"Paul Revere's grave is over there," he offered, unable to resist her enthusiasm as he pointed toward the back of the cemetery. "And John Hancock's is that way."

"Let's go see them!" She took his hand and dragged him in the direction he'd indicated.

He had to laugh out of sheer pleasure at viewing Camille's exuberance. She must have led an unbelievably sheltered life, and he felt a certain thrill himself in being the one to show her things she'd never seen before.

They got sidetracked on the way to Paul Revere when Baylor decided to show her the undistinguished grave of the woman believed to be Mother Goose. The marker had been stolen years before, but Baylor knew the spot.

Camille studied the bare ground with a perplexed expression. "I'm afraid I'm not familiar with Mother Goose," she said at last.

He was floored. "Mother Goose—you know, nursery rhymes?" he prompted. "Hey diddle diddle, the cat and the fiddle? There was an old woman who lived in a shoe?"

She smiled at that, but there was no light of recognition in her eyes.

Abruptly Baylor felt a tremendous anger—not toward Camille, but toward her parents. How could they have done this to their own child? How could they have isolated her so thoroughly from the world? Had she experienced any of the normal joys of childhood—summer camp, or visiting Santa Claus? Had she ever been on a date, for God's sake?

Had she ever—no, probably not.

"Baylor, what's wrong?"

He realized that he'd reached out to touch her cheek, and he felt an overwhelming urge to kiss her moist, full lips, which were parted slightly in surprise. He wanted to be her first lover, to awaken the sensuality he already knew she possessed. But first he wanted to hug the lonely child she must have been, to reassure her that she didn't have to be lonely as long as he was around.

"I was just imagining how it must have been for you growing up," he finally said, telling at least part of the truth. "I'm trying to justify what your parents did to you."

"Did to me? They didn't *do* anything to me. Mostly I did it to myself."

"How?" he asked with more than idle curiosity. "Explain to me how a kid in America can grow up without someone having read them a book of nursery rhymes."

Again she took his hand, and wordlessly she led him to a bench that caught the last of the afternoon sun. "My parents loved me," she said when they were both seated in a bright patch of sunlight. "And I have no doubt that at some point my mother read nursery rhymes to me. I'm also fairly certain I would have shown no interest in them. I was a painfully logical child. I would have known that cats playing fiddles and old women living in shoes were impossible concepts. And if I didn't plague my mother with questions about it, I was probably tearing the book apart trying to figure out how it was bound together."

"But to keep you at home instead of letting you attend school—"

"I tried school—twice. I was bored to tears, even in a class of kids two or three years older than me. I challenged every statement the teacher made. I always wanted to know more than they were willing to teach me. Other children didn't like me. It just didn't work. I was much happier at home, letting my father tutor me at my own pace."

"But were you really happy?"

She smiled fondly. "Sometimes. Father was a hard teacher, and somewhat single-minded about my education, but he opened so many doors for me. He knew I was capable of achieving everything he had and more, so he pushed me to excel. He actually expected me to win a Nobel Prize someday. I wanted that too, once..." She paused, a thoughtful expression on her face.

Baylor absently stroked a strand of her soft brown hair and said nothing.

"Other kids got nursery rhymes and fairy tales at bed-time. Instead my father used to tell me the wonderful things I'd accomplish as a world-class scientist—curing diseases, or sending astronauts to Mars. God, yes, he loved me. They both loved me. It just never occurred to them that my own dreams for the future might not always be the same as theirs..."

"And what are your dreams for the future?" Baylor asked softly.

"You mean, what do I want to be when I grow up?" She laughed self-consciously but then sobered. "I've only recently begun to consider the possibilities, the choices no one ever offered me. I'd like to try writing my book. And then maybe I'd like to be a teacher. Or I'd like to work with schools in developing programs for gifted students. I don't really know, I guess."

"And what do you want on a more personal level?" he couldn't help asking.

She didn't have to think too hard about her answer this time. "I'd like to travel. I'd like to read more of the great literature I only sampled growing up. In the long run, I want what most women want—a husband, kids, a house, a flower garden. I want to have friends and go to parties. I want to learn to cook... I just want to be normal," she added, summing everything up. "That's all I've ever really wanted."

Her wistful expression touched him as nothing else could have. He slid an arm about her shoulders without even thinking twice. He found it hard not to feel close to her when she was opening herself up to him so poignantly. "I had the opposite problem growing up," he said. "I was always *too* normal, *too* average. All I ever wanted was to be exceptional."

"There's no such thing as too normal," she said, leaning her head on his shoulder.

"There is in my family." It occurred to him that she fit against him all too comfortably. He could get used to her warmth next to him. "I grew up in a nest of geniuses," he explained. "I think I told you about my father, the inventor. There's also my mother—she's the mastermind behind countless successful political campaigns. Then there's my sister the brain surgeon and my brother—my baby brother—the engineer who flies all over the world to consult on bridges and dams."

"Good genes, I guess," she said, sounding less impressed than most people did when they learned about his family. But that only made sense, given her own background.

"And then there's me, the black sheep," he said.

Camille was silent for a moment. "What's a 'black sheep'?"

Baylor chuckled. "You do have some interesting holes in your education. That's a disreputable person who doesn't fit in with the rest of the family, the one everyone else is ashamed of."

She stiffened in protest. "Why would they be ashamed of you?" she said, pulling away from him so she could face him.

Now he wished he hadn't gotten her all riled up. He wanted her back, tucked securely against his side. "I made lousy grades. Then I dropped out of college," he explained.

"That's it? For heaven's sake, you made it sound like you'd done something really bad."

"That is bad, in my family. What's worse, I quit school to become a cop—a lowly, blue-collar job. I haven't *distinguished* myself, as my mother says. Making detec-

tive—the youngest detective in the whole damn city—
didn't count." He shook his head, remembering how
proud he'd been when he'd announced the big promo-
tion, and how quickly his parents had deflated that sense
of pride with a few pithy questions about his "earnings
potential" and "standing in the community."

Camille leaned back against him with a thud. "Sounds
like your parents are as rigid as mine were. At least you had
the courage to go your own way, despite their objec-
tions."

"Yeah, well." He shrugged. "Maybe I should have listened to them more than I did. I've about decided I'm not
such a hot cop after all."

"Why?" she asked, sounding genuinely surprised.

He didn't answer her. They sat in silence for a few minutes, surrounded by the peacefulness of the centuries-old
graves.

"I used to think I was a good detective—maybe even a
great one," Baylor said, beginning cautiously. He'd never
confided his doubts aloud to anyone. But he had this feeling Camille might be the one person who'd understand.
They were alike in a lot of ways, he realized. They'd both
had to grow up with tremendous parental pressures. And
they'd both come to question their career paths, with serious consequences.

"What changed your mind?" she asked.

He hesitated. Did he really want to relive the incident
aloud? He decided to circle around it first. "From the time
I walked my first beat, everyone said I had an uncanny
knack for uncovering the true facts of any case."

"And do you?"

He shrugged again. "I had some lucky breaks. And
maybe I was better than the average guy when it came to
seeing the big picture—you know, locking in on inconsis-

tencies, figuring out motives. To me it was like putting together the pieces of a puzzle.''

"Like the wooden elephant," Camille added.

He nodded. "Exactly. People said I had an instinct, a God-given talent for police work. And I believed them. So I played hunches, took chances, and they always seemed to pay off."

"I would think sometimes a detective has to take chances," she said.

"Calculated risks, maybe," he agreed. "But I was too damn cocky." He hesitated, still unsure whether he could relive that cold, horrible night.

"So what happened?" Camille prodded gently.

He took a deep breath and plunged ahead. "Two months ago I was called in to diffuse a . . . situation. This guy was drunk and holding his wife and kid hostage with a gun. I should have gone by the book—there are certain procedures, you see. Instead I trusted my own interpretation of the situation."

"What did you do?" she urged again in her patient, nonthreatening voice.

Again he inhaled deeply, sucking in a little courage. And somehow, the story emerged. With each word, each broken sentence, he relived the incident with frightening intensity. "I was almost sure the man holding the gun was bluffing—but only almost," he said. "I was feeling cocky. So I took a chance I shouldn't have, and I rushed the guy."

"And what happened?" Camille asked breathlessly, clutching his hand.

"He shot wildly. The bullet struck a twenty-two-year-old patrolman." He could feel the blood draining from his face as he spoke the words. The pictures in his mind were still as fresh as they had been two months ago. So much blood.

"Did the patrolman die?" The question was barely whispered.

"No. But he could have. I managed to disarm the gunman, but after that I was too shook-up to be of much help. The next day I tried to turn in my badge. My captain wouldn't accept it. He told me to take a leave of absence instead. But I'm not going back."

Camille's objection was immediate. "You can't give up your career just because of one—"

"One mistake?" he finished for her. "Believe me, I've heard the argument before. And if I thought it was just one unfortunate mistake, I'd be inclined to agree. But it's more than that."

"How so?"

"I've lost something. This knack for ferreting out the truth—call it a gift, call it instinct—whatever it is, if I ever had it, I've lost it."

Chapter Seven

Lost it, my foot, Camille wanted to say. Instinct wasn't something that could just fly out the window. It was a talent that originated in the brain, every bit as real and concrete as her knack for numbers. He could no more lose it than she could lose her ability to solve equations.

As a matter of fact, the intuitive skill Baylor described could be classified as a form of genius. His talent was different from hers in that it was governed by the right brain hemisphere, as opposed to her own left-brain, linear logic. But genius was genius, and it wasn't something that came and went—she should know, as often as she'd tried to wish hers away.

But neither was it infallible, as Baylor had apparently learned through the painful incident he'd just related. One error in judgment, so glaring in the face of his otherwise shining record, had caused him to conclude erroneously that he'd lost his instinct. Typical right-brain logic! she thought with a mental sigh of exasperation.

No matter what he believed, his instinct was still with him, though perhaps it was slightly impaired by the recent blow to his confidence. She could try to explain that, but she doubted he was in any mood to listen to an extended lecture on the cerebrum. Right-brainers generally had to learn things for themselves.

"What makes you conclude you've lost your instinct?" she asked, trying to force him to think through his problem logically.

"You saw how I handled that situation with Milo. I should have used a little more finesse instead of barging in like . . . like Rambo."

"Rambo? The elephant?" she asked, bewildered.

"A tough guy in the movies. Never mind," he added when she looked at him blankly. "The point is, if I was in top form, that punk wouldn't have gotten the best of me."

"But you couldn't have guessed that Milo would push me—"

"That's just it. I should have been able to predict exactly what he'd do. You see? I've lost it," he said again.

She decided to try a different tack. "What do your instincts tell you about me?" she asked. "Did I really steal M23?"

He looked away uncomfortably. "I don't know."

"I know you don't *know*, not for sure. But what do you feel?"

He looked back, gifting her with a half-smile. "I'm having a tough time thinking of you as a thief."

"But you don't trust that feeling?"

The small smile faded. "Not entirely."

"Well this time your instinct is right on target," she replied triumphantly. "Of course," she added with a sigh, "I could be lying, couldn't I?"

"That's right." He stared at her, his expression serious. He reached up to softly brush his knuckles against her bruised cheek, the caress somehow a silent apology for the fact that he couldn't give her his whole trust.

His eyes remained locked on hers for an uncomfortable length of time. She thought about looking away to ease the strange tension that had come between them, but she couldn't seem to make herself break the eye contact. By the time she realized he was slowly closing the distance between them, it was too late to do anything except let him kiss her or escape.

She chose the latter, shying away like a skittish filly, then popping onto her feet as if she'd been ejected from a toaster. "Look, there's no more need to pretend you're attracted to me," she said in a too-practical tone. "We both know why you followed me in the first place. Now—" Her voice became falsely bright. "I'm going to see Paul Revere." She headed toward the back of the cemetery without waiting for a response from Baylor.

It wasn't that she didn't want to kiss him—not at all. But she was oddly vulnerable right now, having revealed so much of herself to him, and she simply wasn't ready to open up any further. She was starting to feel something for Baylor—something fragile and fluttery, like the new, wet wings of a butterfly just emerging from its cocoon. But like a butterfly, she needed time to adjust to her new wings before she tried to fly with them.

She wanted so much to believe that he'd tried to kiss her out of simple attraction. She wanted to believe that he would treat these brand-new emotions of hers with the utmost care. But his motives had been tainted with deception from the beginning, and she wasn't altogether sure he wasn't still toying with her.

She led the way to the small monument marking Paul Revere's final resting place, feeling Baylor's eyes on her all the while. She silently read the inscription, then touched the cool marble with the pads of her fingers.

"There's another inscription on the back," Baylor said, walking around to the other side of the monument.

Why would anyone inscribe the *back* of a grave marker? she wondered as she stepped around to where Baylor stood, then bent over to peer where he indicated. "Where? I don't see anything." When she straightened and turned, she found herself imprisoned in his arms.

He smiled playfully. "I've got you this time."

"And just what do you plan to do with me?" she said in a defiant, breathless rush of words.

"You already know."

She looked left, then right, hoping an inquisitive tourist or two might cool Baylor's sudden ardor. But they were quite alone in that part of the cemetery, shielded from view by the monument.

Once more she tried to protest, but he cut off her words by taking swift charge of her mouth with his. The kiss was hard, demanding, and irrefutably possessive, without even a pretense of gentleness.

Every rational objection she'd had disappeared on the breeze, and she lost herself to a host of novel sensations. Baylor's kiss reached far beyond her mouth and all the way to the bottom of some deep, mysterious well inside her. Then the well seemed to overflow, flooding every corner of her body with heat.

His tongue made a tentative foray into her mouth. She welcomed it boldly, savoring the feelings created by this new give and take. He insinuated his knee between her legs, bringing their bodies into closer contact. Whether by accident or intention, his thigh pushed intimately against

her, sending shock waves of awareness streaking through
her every which way.

It was all so new, and yet in some odd way familiar, as
if buried somewhere deep in her brain, her inherited mat-
ing instincts, dormant all these years, were coming to life
and letting her know this was right.

"Does this feel like I'm pretending?" he murmured
against her lips before claiming them once again.

No, this is all too real, she admitted silently. However
else he might have misled her, his attraction to her was
solid, as real as the hard arousal she could sense pressing
against her. Part of her was relieved that she hadn't mis-
read the signals she'd picked up since the moment of their
first meeting. But a certain wariness was creeping up on
her, too, as she acknowledged where all this could easily
lead.

Benumbed as she was, she forced herself to close her lips
against his and turn her head. "Aren't we going to attract
unwanted attention?" she asked. "Or does everyone act
this way in public?"

Denied access to her mouth, he made do with nuzzling
her hair. "No one's watching."

"How do you know?" she objected, steeling herself
against the wave of sensations caused by the tip of his
tongue teasing her ear.

"Then let's go home."

"What about the Freedom Trail?" she asked weakly,
though plaques and old buildings didn't hold the appeal
they had a while ago.

"Another day," he promised, easing himself away from
her and smoothing her windblown hair.

The short walk to the subway was accomplished in a
dazed silence. But once inside the Park Street station, the

elbow-to-elbow rush-hour crowd did a lot toward alleviating the sensuous spell that had woven itself around them.

Camille wedged herself between two passive commuters and proceeded to gaze out the window at the tunnel's dim lights. Baylor took a seat across from her. As the train lurched into motion, he thought about the way he'd kissed her and knew he'd gotten carried away in those few mindless moments of passion. He'd taken her too far, too fast. He had to keep reminding himself she was innocent, despite the way she practically ignited the moment he touched her.

He finally spoke his mind when they were away from the subway and walking back toward the car. "I'm not planning to drag you home and jump you."

She looked at him then, startled out of her quiet mood. "Jump me?"

"Take you to bed," he clarified.

"Oh. Am I supposed to be relieved or disappointed?"

He couldn't help but laugh. "It'd be good for my ego if you were disappointed, but I suspect you're a bit relieved."

"I think I'm a little of both. This is all ... I'm not very ... what I mean is—"

"I think I know," he interrupted, placing what was meant to be a comforting hand on her shoulder. "You don't have to explain."

"You *know*?" she repeated, shaking off his touch. "Just what has Paul told you about me, anyway?"

Again Baylor laughed. "Nothing of a personal nature, I promise. I'm just making an educated guess."

She made no reply to that, giving him a skeptical sideways glance that neither confirmed nor denied his suspicions regarding her level of experience.

* * *

A truce had been called. At least, it seemed that way to Camille during the next two days. The hours she spent with Baylor were a glorious time in some respects. The two of them talked a great deal. They prepared meals together—or rather, Baylor cooked and Camille mostly burned things and endured his good-natured teasing. They defeated each other at chess and Trivial Pursuit. They watched late-night TV, another new experience for her. But they didn't touch.

It was as if they'd silently agreed to put their budding physical involvement on hold. The time simply wasn't right for further intimacy. Camille suspected it wouldn't be, until the matter of her guilt or innocence was firmly established, until the doubt and mistrust that plagued them could be put to rest. That would happen only when they recovered the diskettes.

She should have been anxious for In-Ho to call—and she was. But a part of her wanted to stay in the warm cocoon created by the waiting, where she and Baylor could continue to laugh and play games, where Paul's accusations seemed far removed, where she could pretend that Baylor *did* trust her. It was a comfortable limbo that demanded very little of her.

When the call finally came, early the following Friday morning, Camille greeted it with both anticipation and trepidation. Baylor was in the shower. Still wearing his pajamas, she answered the phone with a shaky voice, hoping it wasn't Paul—or worse, someone like Baylor's mother who would scarcely understand Camille's presence in his apartment at seven a.m.

"I'm calling about the disks," In-Ho said without introduction.

"Yes. The reward still stands," Camille responded, her pulse pounding in her ears.

Baylor, who had apparently heard the phone ring, came out of the bathroom in nothing but a towel. She gave him a nod, trying not to let herself be distracted by his beautifully carved bareness. She was tense enough.

She tipped the receiver out so he could lean closer and hear. The scent of soap and menthol shaving cream teased her senses, much to the detriment of her already frayed nerves.

"Listen, you can have the box," In-Ho was saying. "For free. I don't want any more trouble."

Camille exchanged a glance with Baylor, to confirm that he'd heard the same thing she had.

"He's afraid we'll turn him in to the police, and he'll have his parole revoked," Baylor whispered.

Camille nodded, then spoke to In-Ho again. "Where would you like to meet?"

There was a pause. Baylor furiously scribbled something on the back of an envelope and handed it to Camille. "Insist on a very public place," the message read.

Camille suggested the only such place that came to mind. "How about the Public Garden?"

"Too many people know me around there," In-Ho replied. "I'd like to go some place where the other Dawgs won't see me. If Milo finds out what I'm doing I'll be dead meat. What about Quincy Market?" he suggested. "Outside, by the Bull Carts on the south side. This morning? At ten?"

Baylor nodded, indicating that was acceptable.

"All right," Camille agreed. She hung up, trembling with relief. She exchanged a triumphant grin with Baylor, then impulsively threw her arms around his neck in an unfettered reaction of pure joy. "It's over," she said, brushing her cheek against his freshly shaven face.

He tensed almost imperceptibly, then relaxed and returned her hug in kind, running his firm, warm hands up and down her back. "It's not over till the fat lady sings," he murmured.

"What?" She turned her head until she was nose to nose with him—almost mouth to mouth. Suddenly she didn't care who the fat lady was or how she fit into the scheme of things. The truce was over, and that occupied her full attention.

Camille's breath came in short little gasps as she stood in his arms, frozen with indecision. Pressed against his bare chest, she was excruciatingly aware of how little separated their bodies, and how small a space separated their lips. All she had to do was lean forward an inch....

Before she could, however, he loosened his hold on her, then grasped her shoulders and firmly put some distance between them. His lips were pressed firmly together in a grim line.

"What's wrong?" she asked in an embarrassingly breathy whisper.

"Nothing. I just shouldn't have come out here dressed, or rather *un*dressed, like this." He looked down at the precariously draped towel, then back up at her, his grimness giving way to an affectionate smile. "I forget sometimes how innocent you are." Then he turned away from her and started for the bedroom.

She resisted the urge to retort. *Innocent.* She was that, all right, and it was a tedious condition at her age. She intended to put an end to it soon.

Baylor sat on a bench on the mall outside Quincy Market, once again neutral in his faded jeans and a cream-colored sweater. He'd taken the additional precaution of wearing sunglasses, and he kept his nose buried in a newspaper. The paper had a small tear in it, however, so he could keep watch over Camille.

She'd blossomed over the last few days—there was no other word for it. She hardly resembled the drab, forlorn creature he'd first seen in the bank lobby.

This morning she'd pulled yet another outfit from her seemingly bottomless shopping bags: stylish acid-washed jeans and a blue-and-white striped blouse. Her large hazel eyes, enhanced slightly with a bit of makeup, sparkled with anticipation and her cheeks glowed pink. She'd tamed her chestnut hair into a saucy ponytail and tied it with a blue scarf.

The end result of her efforts gave her the appearance of a brightly wrapped package, he thought. He looked forward to unwrapping her, and he would—soon.

He watched appreciatively as she strolled through colorful Bull Carts under the canopies, examining handmade jewelry, intricately tie-dyed clothing, and other wares of local artisans. She pulled some money out of her homely backpack and bought a pastry, then ended up feeding most of it to a crowd of hungry pigeons who knew an easy mark when they saw one.

She played it cool for a good half hour after their appointed meeting time with In-Ho. But when it became apparent the boy wasn't going to show, she ambled over to the bench and sank down next to Baylor, a picture of pure exasperation. "What do you suppose happened to him?"

Baylor laid down the newspaper, feeling every bit as frustrated as Camille sounded. "He might have changed his mind. Or he might have—wait, what's *that*?"

She looked in the direction he pointed. They both stared at a young man wearing daringly cut dress pants, a pin-striped shirt, maroon suspenders and a paisley tie. He looked a little worse for wear—one of the suspenders was unhooked, the tie was askew, and he held a cloth of some kind to his face. His short, black hair stuck straight up in uneven tufts.

"My heavens, it's In-Ho," Camille confirmed. "I never would have recognized him." She was already up off the bench and heading toward him. Baylor followed, but he hung back, waiting for Camille to make the initial contact and signal him that it was all right to approach. He watched the two exchange a few words. It was apparent that In-Ho had been on the losing end of someone's fist. He was suffering from a nosebleed, and the first signs of a purplish bruise were appearing along his jaw.

Camille fussed over him a little—she seemed to be a natural-born fusser—then signaled to Baylor. "Milo got the disks away from him," she announced.

"He got me when I was coming out of my apartment building," In-Ho explained anxiously. "I should have been more careful, I guess. I thought he wasn't interested in the disks anymore."

"Let's go sit down and have some coffee," Camille suggested practically, though she wilted with disappointment bordering on despair. "Then we can hear the whole story."

"Okay," In-Ho agreed tamely enough, to Baylor's amazement, "but I can't hang around long. I got a job interview at eleven."

That explained the clothes, Baylor thought. The kid looked almost respectable.

"What kind of job?" Camille asked as they made their way inside Quincy Market and found a table in the rotunda.

"With the city. Something to do with translating, 'cause I'm what they call bilingual." He said this with a touch of pride. "If I apply now, they can hire me when I turn eighteen in a couple of months. My boss in maintenance put in a good word for me.''

''I'll get the coffee,'' Baylor announced, since Camille and In-Ho seemed to be getting along like old chums. By the time he returned with three steaming cups, the two of them were deep in conversation.

''So,'' Baylor interrupted as he sat down. ''Is it common for members of the Dawgs to work for the city?''

Camille gave him a disapproving frown at the confrontational question.

In-Ho shrugged. ''My sister said she'd throw me out if I didn't stay in school or get a full-time job, one or the other. Anyway,'' he mumbled, ''maybe I don't want to be a Dawg forever.''

''Why not?'' Baylor asked suspiciously.

''My parole officer said if I get caught hanging out with the gang I'll go back to detention—jail, maybe, at my age. 'Sides, it's gotten too dangerous ever since Milo came along and started bossing us around. He takes too many chances.''

''Is he one of the organizers?'' Baylor asked.

In-Ho shook his head with a laugh. ''The leaders don't like him either. He's been running a few operations on his own, without cutting them in. He doesn't follow orders very good.''

Baylor took a long sip of coffee. ''The, uh, leaders, will they let you leave the gang?''

In-Ho lowered his voice. ''I cut a deal. They'll let me out if I help them get rid of Milo.''

''Get *rid* of Milo?'' Camille repeated, paling slightly.

The boy rolled his eyes. ''I don't mean waste him. Get him out of the way, that's all.''

''Oh, you mean in jail,'' she said, nodding. ''When he stands trial for that armed robbery charge?''

Baylor narrowed his eyes at Camille, wondering again where she got her information. She'd unwittingly hit on something this time. "Thinking of turning a little state's evidence, In-Ho?" he asked on a hunch.

"No," the teenager said, shaking his head vehemently, realizing he'd said too much. "Listen, thanks for the coffee but I gotta go—"

"What's the hurry?" Baylor asked, clamping a firm hand on In-Ho's shoulder. "Look, kid, I've got a proposition for you. Help us get the disks back and I'll help you strike a deal with the D.A. You might not even have to testify, if you can provide some other evidence that'll put Milo away, and you'll be granted immunity."

In-Ho shook his head in denial. "I wasn't there. I didn't see nothing, you hear? I—" He froze, his eyes riveted over Camille's shoulder.

"What is it?" Baylor asked, releasing his grip on In-Ho and peering down the corridor in the direction the boy was staring. A flash of white blond hair and a green fatigue jacket appeared among the crowd, then vanished just as quickly, answering Baylor's question.

"He must have followed me," In-Ho said, reflexively rising from his chair. "I'm getting out of here, and if you're smart you'll do the same." With that he bolted, melting into the milieu with amazing speed.

Baylor stood and grasped Camille's hand. "We're about to have company. Let's take In-Ho's advice. We'll see if we can't turn the tables on Milo the way you did me a few days ago."

"You mean give him the slip and then tail him?" she said.

"Right." Baylor couldn't help grinning at the terminology she'd obviously picked up from last night's gangster movie they'd watched on TV. He got a firm grip on her hand and led her through the crowd on the other side of the rotunda from Milo. He then positioned them behind a balloon stand.

They watched as their adversary ambled closer. He looked nonchalantly toward the rotunda, froze, then swiveled his head left, right, and over his shoulder. He started toward the open space at a determined clip.

"He's lost sight of us," Baylor said. "He wasn't expecting us to move that quickly."

"But he's coming this way. I'm scared. Baylor, let's get out of here."

"Shh. Just stand behind me. Nothing's going to happen." He unfolded his newspaper and leaned his shoulder against a support column in a well-practiced pose.

"I don't like this," Camille said from behind him. "What's he doing?"

"Shh. He's passing about twenty feet away. He's looking and . . . he doesn't see us. He's moving on."

Camille expelled a long breath. "Now we follow him?" she asked. "But how will we get the disks back?"

"They're probably in his pocket right now. He hasn't had time to stash them anywhere, not if he tailed In-Ho. All we have to do is seize the right opportunity." They waited until the beacon of white hair was well ahead of them before following.

Camille clutched Baylor's hand in a death grip. "What sort of opportunity?"

"I'll know it when I see it."

They watched from behind a flower cart as Milo worked his way down the row of tradespeople under the canopies outside the market. Though he pretended interest in the merchants' wares, his eyes were constantly scanning the area around him.

Baylor noted the presence of a uniformed policewoman making a casual tour of the area. He knew her vaguely—her name was Tracy something. Her presence was one added point in their favor.

After a while, Milo seemed to give up searching for them, and he started paying more attention to the items for sale. He spent a long while with a jewelry artisan, looking at various necklaces of silver and turquoise.

"What's he doing?" Camille asked.

Baylor shrugged. "Shopping, I guess. The kid probably makes more money than he knows how to spend."

Milo pulled some bills out of his back pocket, having apparently made a choice. The artist smiled graciously as she wrapped his purchase meticulously in tissue paper and placed it in a gift box. At the same time, Milo was casually stuffing a handful of silver jewelry into his jacket pocket.

Camille gasped. "Did you see that?"

Baylor's mind was racing. This was exactly the chance he'd been looking for. Within the span of fifteen seconds he came up with a plan—a precarious one, but it might be their only chance. "We have to move fast," he told Camille in a commanding voice. He pointed to the policewoman. "Go get the cop over there and bring her over to the jeweler's cart. Then follow my lead, okay?"

Though she appeared confused, Camille gave a quick nod of assent, then darted off toward the female officer, who was standing next to a tree and looking bored.

Baylor, meanwhile, made contact with the jewelry artisan. "That blond kid just ripped you off," he told the woman urgently, praying his timing was right. "I'll help you detain him. A cop is on the way."

The artist lurched to angry attention. "You're damn right I'll detain him," she said, sliding off her chair and stalking toward Milo, outrage personified. Baylor sprinted past the two carts next door so he could cut off Milo's most likely avenue of escape. He slid into position just as the jeweler confronted the boy with a series of loud accusations, complete with a kick in the shins.

"Here now, stop that," said the officer as she arrived on the scene with Camille right behind. "What's going on here?"

Milo turned to run, but Baylor blocked his path.

The artisan pointed to Baylor. "He saw this kid steal my jewelry."

The policewoman eyed Baylor curiously, then smiled when she recognized him as a fellow officer.

"First the kid stole a box from this woman's backpack," Baylor improvised, pointing to Camille. "She ran to get you while I kept an eye on him. That's when I saw him steal the jewelry, too. I'm on a leave of absence, so I couldn't make the arrest myself," he told her, anticipating her next question.

The officer spoke briefly into her two-way radio, then turned her attention to a defiant but frightened Milo, who for once didn't have a single smart comeback. She gave him a skeptical once-over.

In a matter of seconds she had him spread-eagled against the back of a park bench and was patting him down. The body search produced a tangle of silver jewelry and, to Baylor's immense relief, the white box of diskettes.

"You want to press charges?" the policewoman asked the jeweler.

"You bet I do. That's the third time this month I've been ripped off."

"I'll have to keep the jewelry for evidence, then. Okay, kid, you're under arrest." She read him his rights in a monotone, then turned to Camille. "What about you? Do you want to press charges?"

"No," Camille answered decisively as Baylor nodded his approval. "No harm done. I just want my box back."

The officer shrugged. "Okay." She handed the white box to Camille, who clutched it as if it were full of diamonds.

Two more uniforms arrived as backup. Baylor patiently answered interminable questions. Camille did a lot of nodding and agreeing. Finally, after what seemed an eternity, Milo was carted off.

"You okay?" Baylor asked Camille when they found themselves alone again.

She took a deep breath and sank onto the nearest bench. "I don't know. It all happened so fast I didn't have time to think about what we were doing. I can see now where you got your reputation." She paused, then turned to look at him with an impish smile. "Are you sure you've lost your instinct?"

Too antsy to sit down, he moved to stand behind her and rest his hands on her shoulders. He *had* felt a small surge of instinct taking over during the last few minutes. "Maybe it's still there, somewhere," he said on a hopeful note.

"Why didn't Milo argue with us?" she asked, worrying her bottom lip with her teeth. "We didn't exactly tell the whole truth."

"Milo knows to keep his mouth shut when he's under arrest. Besides, if the real story comes out, he could be charged with kidnapping, assault, extortion, maybe even attempted murder. He did push us off a second-story loading bay."

Camille shivered, again remembering that cold, black water. "You think it's better we don't reveal all the facts?"

"It would have taken hours to unravel the whole story, and then they would have kept the disks for evidence," Baylor rationalized.

"But what if that measly theft isn't enough to keep him in jail?"

"It's enough for a while," Baylor answered, absently stroking the back of her neck with his thumbs. Her skin was satiny smooth, but the muscles underneath were tense with accumulated stress. "He committed a crime while he was out on bond. That should count for something. Meanwhile, I'll have a chat with the D.A. about In-Ho, among other things."

She seemed to relax a little as he massaged away the tightness. "I guess the important thing is that we got the disks back," she said, looking down at the box she held in a white-knuckle grip. "Oh, Baylor, I can't wait any longer. Let's go find a computer, and I'll prove once and for all that these disks contain nothing but a bunch of silly notes." She opened the box and showed him the disks themselves. "Look at the labels. They say Personal Notes, and then the dates. See?"

Baylor gave them a cursory examination. "That's what they say, all right."

"And I suppose you're thinking that I could have stuck any kind of label on the M23 disks, right?" she asked indignantly, closing the box.

He gave her shoulder one final reassuring squeeze. He wished he could tell her he trusted her. He wanted to. He almost could. "Come on, let's end the suspense once and for all. There's a computer store on Washington Street. Maybe we can talk them into lending us a machine."

"I can't *believe* you still think I'm a thief," she stormed as they made their way up the sidewalk toward the computer store. "After all we've been through—"

"I can't help it," he said defensively. "I'm trained to be suspicious."

"You're not using your head," she grumped. "If these disks contained M23, do you think I'd just meekly show you what's on them?"

"You haven't showed me yet," he pointed out.

The store was not far, but even the short walk exhausted Camille. She was at the end of her stress rope. She hadn't been sleeping well the past few nights. This morning's anxiety had sapped what little energy she had left.

As soon as they entered the store, Camille had a quick look around until she spotted a familiar model, a newer version of her own computer. "That one," she said, pointing to it. "I also need a WriteMaster word-processing program."

"You sit down," Baylor said, placing her firmly in a chair that was part of an office furniture display. "You seem a little shaky. I'll talk to a salesperson and arrange something."

While she waited, she looked around the spacious store, thinking she'd never seen a place quite like it before. Personal computers had come a long way since she'd acquired hers several years ago. She'd need to buy a new one if she wanted to write her book.

She gazed around her with increasing interest at all the different styles of machines. Should she get a hard disk? she wondered. A color monitor? She saw a display of diskettes on sale and found herself wandering over to see if they offered the brand she liked, the kind she'd always bought from the commissary at Easterwood.

"There you are," she murmured to herself, absently picking up one of the new white boxes and noting that the price was much lower than what she'd paid in the past. She'd have to remember this place—"Oh!"

A pair of steel-gripped hands had grasped her shoulders from behind. "What are you doing?"

"Oh, it's you," she said, relieved. For a moment she'd thought Milo had escaped the police and was coming to get her. She turned to face Baylor. "I was just checking the price on these—" She stopped cold when she read the suspicion in his vivid green eyes. She looked down at the two boxes of diskettes she held, then back up at him. "You thought I was trying to switch disks on you?" she said, horrified.

He didn't respond. He didn't have to.

"Darn it—*damn* it, Baylor, you're going to apologize when you see what's on these disks. Can we use the computer?"

"The salesman is setting it up now," he said, his jaw clenched.

"Good. Let's get this over with."

They stood staring at each other until the computer and software were ready. Then Camille sat confidently in front of the keyboard and inserted a random disk from her box into the drive. The screen flashed her a message: "Software does not support this format."

Something wasn't right.

She tried another disk, only to get the same message. Her hands started to shake. "This is WriteMaster II?" she asked the salesman, who hovered nearby.

"That's right."

Her heart fluttered madly. She exited the word processing program and returned to the main operating system. Then she requested a directory of the files on her disks. The machine hummed for a moment, then began printing the files on the screen, one after another.

Camille felt the blood draining from her face. Every file was prefaced by the same three digits: M-2-3.

Chapter Eight

"Care to comment on that?" Baylor's voice was cold as December.

Camille forced herself to take slow, deep breaths. This couldn't be happening. But of course it was. The damning evidence flashed green and menacing from the computer screen. What could she say about it that wouldn't sound ludicrous?

Wordlessly, with slow, measured movements, she ejected the disk, put it in its plastic sleeve and returned it to the box. She handed the box to Baylor without meeting his gaze.

Baylor thanked the salesman for his trouble, though Camille wasn't aware of what he said. Her surroundings had ceased to exist. Moving with all the grace of a marionette, she allowed Baylor to usher her out of the store with a firm hand on her arm.

They said nothing on the way to the subway station, nor during the short train ride to Charlestown. It was only when they arrived at Baylor's car that she could manage a few words.

"Where are we going?"

He looked at her, seemingly startled that she had spoken. "I'm taking these disks to Paul before anything else can happen to them. As for you ... you can go wherever you want."

She could hardly believe what she was hearing. "You'd let me walk away?"

"All I want to do is return M23 to Paul," Baylor answered woodenly. "I don't particularly want to see you go to jail. I can tell him you slipped away again. Lord knows he'll believe it." He stared down at the pavement.

Camille dropped her backpack to the ground with a thud. "Now you listen to me, Baylor Pierce," she said with a sudden burst of ferocity, advancing on him until she was nearly nose to collarbone. "I have no intention of going to jail, and I will not sneak off like I have something to hide while you and Paul condemn me without a trial."

Baylor was shaking his head. "Don't, Camille. Don't dig yourself in any deeper."

She assessed the closed, hard expression on his face and snorted with disgust. "You wouldn't even listen to an explanation, would you?"

"Why, do you have one?" he challenged.

"No," she admitted, then added firmly, "but I intend to find one." She picked up her pack and stood resolutely by the passenger door of the car, waiting for him to unlock it. He hesitated, finally deciding he couldn't drive off and leave her standing there. She had the right to face Paul and plead her case, weak though it was. He climbed behind the steering wheel and unlocked her door from the inside.

"Why are you so mad?" she asked, buckling her seat belt after he'd screeched out of the parking space. "I'd think you'd be ecstatic at the prospect of returning to Paul victorious, with the precious M23 in tow."

"Why am I mad? You made a fool of me," he seethed. "You led me on a wild-goose chase all over Boston. You slept under my roof, ate my food—I almost got killed because of you. I *trusted* you, so much that I told you things I've never told anyone. You let me kiss you, for crying out loud. You wonder why I'm mad?"

"You never trusted me," she said quietly. "Up to the very last moment you had doubts. If you'd just listened to your instinct—"

"Leave my damned instinct out of this. I don't need instinct when I have cold, hard evidence."

She didn't know what to say to that. No amount of reassurance from her would convince him of her innocence at this point.

Baylor clenched his jaw and concentrated on his driving, silent like a volcano after a particularly violent eruption. He felt betrayed, by Camille and by his own feelings. Why had he let himself get so close to her? Why had he allowed himself to care about her? Even now his fickle instincts were telling him she was innocent, but such faulty signals had to be the result of his emotions overriding his common sense.

He slid his gaze in her direction. She looked pale and sad, wearing the expression of a child who'd lost her favorite toy. How could she possibly be a thief? But she was—there was no denying the evidence now. She couldn't have committed the crime strictly for personal gain, he caught himself thinking. There must be some other factors involved. What could have made her resort to larceny?

She turned her head, catching his gaze. "Even now your instinct tells you I'm not guilty, doesn't it?"

He started, surprised by her accuracy. He thought carefully before answering. "I was thinking that you must have had a compelling reason to do what you did. Did someone force you to do it?"

The question was met with stubborn silence.

"Did you need money?" he tried again. "If you'll just tell me why, I'll try to help you. I'm sure Paul will go easy on you if you would just explain to him—"

She made a squeaky sound of exasperation and clenched her hands together in her lap, as if she were struggling to resist the temptation to strangle him. "Okay, forget instinct. Let's try logic instead. Did it ever occur to you, for instance, that someone set me up?"

"Who?" he shot back. "And why? The possibility did occur to me—some time ago, as a matter of fact. I dismissed it. In order to set you up, someone would have had to know of your plans to leave Easterwood. You left without telling anyone."

He had a point, she thought, falling silent.

"You can tell me the truth," he said in a gentle voice. "I'm on your side, don't you know that? I'll stand by you—"

"Oh, give it a rest, would you?" she snapped, repeating a particularly apt phrase she'd learned from television. She folded her arms and stared out the window. She needed to stop feeling sorry for herself and put her brains to work. She could have used Baylor's help, but since he obviously wasn't going to cooperate, she'd have to rely on her own gray matter.

Someone had set her up. That had to be the answer. But as Baylor pointed out, who could have known she was going to run away? Had she accidentally sent out subliminal signals, alerting someone to her departure? And who despised her enough to frame her? Who hated her that much? As far as she knew, she didn't have any enemies.

She approached it from another angle. Who would have the know-how to gain access to M23's data files and manipulate them? The cast of suspects narrowed considerably, for security in the Nuclear Physics division was extremely tight. Only four people had access to the computer where M23's data was stored—Paul, Nita, Larry and herself.

She considered Larry first, the only technician in the complex with high-level security clearance. The man was a master at breaking entry codes and such. If anyone could outsmart the antitheft programming and wipe out the sensitive data files, Larry could. But what reason would he have to perpetrate such a crime?

Camille shook her head. Larry wasn't above fixing parking tickets, but he didn't seem ambitious or hateful enough to orchestrate such an elaborate scheme. Besides, how and why would he have planted the backup disks among her belongings?

Who next—Nita? Camille laughed inwardly at the very thought of Paul's devoted secretary breaking into a computer and stealing data. The woman was a technophobe. She was intimidated by the electric coffeepot and positively terrified of computers. Once Camille had tried to show Nita how easy it was to type and correct letters with a word processor. The poor woman's hands had frozen above the keyboard. She'd been petrified to push a single button, as if she'd thought the machine would explode, and no amount of coaxing from Camille would alleviate the irrational fear.

So Nita was out. That left Paul.

Camille squirmed in her seat, uncomfortable with the possibility that her former boss could be so dishonest. He'd been like an older brother to her these last three years. He'd taken care of things for her when her parents had died. He'd held her hand and guided her through her first exciting months working on M23. Could he have turned on her so maliciously?

She attempted to detach herself emotionally and consider the facts. It wasn't inconceivable that he could steal from Easterwood. He'd often expressed dissatisfaction toward the company, saying he didn't get paid what he was worth for his single-minded devotion to his work. But to sell M23 to a competitor would effectively end his work on the project. Camille had a hard time believing he'd do that.

And even if she could believe it, she couldn't stomach the notion that he would deliberately shift blame for the theft onto her. Then again, she thought with a sour taste in her mouth, he'd been awfully quick to accuse her. Unreasonably quick.

By the time Baylor was guiding the sedan into Easterwood's visitor's parking lot, Camille hadn't reached any conclusions. This puzzle made her think again of the wooden elephant, whose secret still eluded her.

They entered through the familiar front doors of the main building. The receptionist, a forbidding woman affectionately known as The Palace Guard, looked on sternly as Camille flashed her employee badge and Baylor signed in on a clipboard. Camille half expected a cadre of security guards to descend the moment she showed her face, but the receptionist hardly even blinked at her. Paul must have kept her disappearance hush-hush.

She led the way along one hallway after another, then down two floors in an elevator, then through several more corridors into the bowels of the complex, where the Nuclear Physics division was housed behind a set of thick steel doors. Two video cameras panned the area. An electronic keypad required a numerical code for entrance.

Camille punched in the familiar numbers. She received an Access Denied message from the small screen above the keypad. "Paul switched codes on me," she grumbled as she picked up the house phone and dialed Paul's extension. She handed the receiver to Baylor, not trusting herself to speak civilly to Paul just now.

"Buzz me in," Baylor said into the phone. "I've recovered your M23. And I've got Camille with me."

Even standing some distance away from Baylor, she could hear the unrestrained whoop of victory coming through the earpiece. Baylor winced and pulled the receiver away from his ear, then waited until a buzzing sound signaled that the door was open before hanging up and guiding Camille inside.

Paul strode toward them at a determined pace as the steel doors closed behind them with a final-sounding clang. He flashed a toothy smile as he reached to accept the white box Baylor held out for him. "Is it all here?" he asked, opening the box and peering curiously at the disks inside.

Baylor shrugged. "You'll have to check that yourself. Those disks have been through quite an ordeal."

"I'll look at them right away." Paul then turned on Camille with the swiftness of a cobra. His smile vanished, replaced by a twisted grimace of such malevolence it made Camille flinch. He pointed his finger in her face. "So help me, Camille, if even one sector of this data is damaged or missing, I'm holding you responsible. I may see you in jail yet. It's inconceivable that you could do such a thing, and yet I'm holding the evidence in my hand. Thank God your father isn't alive to see—"

"If he were alive," she interrupted, "my father would not allow you to condemn me without a full investigation. You, Paul, if anyone, should know not to jump to conclusions."

"Tell me, Camille," Paul said through clenched teeth, "what other conclusion could I possibly reach? You disappear, the project disappears, and Baylor finds the disks in your belongings—"

"I was set up."

"By whom?" Paul demanded, advancing on her as if he might actually do her physical harm. "Who knew you were going to fly the coop? Surely you can come up with a better story than that."

To her surprise, Baylor stepped in front of her as if to shield her from Paul's wrath. "Take it easy, Paul," he said evenly. "She's been through a lot."

"Well so have I," Paul boomed.

"If we could just all sit down and discuss this calmly—" Camille started to say.

"Oh, don't worry, you'll get your chance to talk." Paul narrowed his eyes menacingly at her, then turned his gaze on Baylor. "Take her into my office while I check these disks out," he said before turning and disappearing around a corner toward the computer room.

"Sure you don't want to clap the handcuffs on me now?" Camille groused as she led the way to Paul's office.

"Count your blessings," Baylor grumbled back. "At least he hasn't called the police. You may get off lucky. He doesn't want any publicity."

"At least if I'm arrested I'll get a trial," she shot back, thoroughly disgusted with both men. They acted as if they didn't share a brain cell between them. They both had dismissed her theory that she'd been framed simply because it didn't seem likely. But was it any more plausible that *she* would steal M23? So far no one had assigned her a reasonable motive.

Maybe when they all had a chance to talk, reason would prevail, she hoped as she sat in one of the leather upholstered chairs facing Paul's glossy walnut desk.

Baylor took the seat next to her. "Are you all right?" he asked.

"Spare me your concern. No, I'm not all right. I'm madder than hell and I have a headache. I'm also—" she stopped when the office door opened and Nita sidled in with a plate of plastic-wrapped sandwiches and two small cans of apple juice.

Nita looked at both of the room's occupants, then nodded politely, her face revealing no emotion. "Paul said he'll be here in a few more minutes," she said, setting the plate on the desk. "I thought you might be hungry, Camille. You know how you get when you don't eat properly."

"I've been eating just fine," Camille replied, resenting Nita's implication that she didn't have enough sense to eat a balanced meal unless someone provided it for her.

Nita's face fell at the sharp retort.

"I *am* hungry, though," Camille added guiltily, taking what she thought was a turkey sandwich. "Thank you."

"Oh, Camille, honey—" The older woman's voice cracked. "I just can't believe—"

"Everyone keeps saying they can't believe I did it," Camille said bitterly. "Then why are you all taking my guilt for granted?"

Nita and Baylor exchanged a silent glance, but neither made any reply. Camille returned the unopened sandwich to the tray. She couldn't have swallowed a bite.

For almost thirty minutes the three sat in silence in Paul's office. When Paul finally reappeared, Nita took out a notepad and began to scribble in it—the kangaroo court reporter, Camille mused grimly.

"Everything looks to be in order," Paul announced, "though of course I won't know for sure until I make a more detailed search through the data files. Apparently the antitheft device written into the program didn't destroy the data when it was transferred, as it should have. You're lucky, Camille."

"Wish I could agree with you," she said, staring up at the ceiling.

"You're lucky because I'm not going to press charges. Just return the physical components and you can walk out of here a free woman. I won't even require an explanation from you, although you owe me one."

"I don't have the physical components," she said evenly.

"Then where are they? At least two people saw you mail that package—"

"Just because I carried a package to the mail room doesn't mean I knew what was in it."

Baylor interrupted at that point, explaining about Camille's astounding recall of the address on the package, their subsequent trip to the Somerville post office, and what they'd discovered.

"I couldn't have cleaned out the box myself," Camille added, anticipating Paul's next accusation. "I spent the whole morning in a bakery."

Paul looked at Baylor for confirmation.

Baylor shrugged uneasily. "She couldn't remember the name of the bakery," he said, staring down at his tennis shoes.

Camille leaned her head back and closed her eyes. This was a nightmare. When she opened them again, Paul was staring at her, his gaze as sharp as needles.

"Well?" he said. "Are you going to continue this ridiculous charade? Why don't you just admit—"

"I didn't do it." She felt tears of frustration pressing hotly against the back of her eyes. Determined to hold herself together, she took several deep breaths and swallowed the lump in her throat. In a few moments she was ready to make one last stab at clearing herself. "Paul, I know this is asking a lot, but could you assume for a moment that I *didn't* do it? Just out of respect for the three years of solid work we did together. Could you at least consider other possibilities?"

Paul sighed. "Camille—"

"Just hear me out," she said, cutting off his objection. "Pretend this is a mystery—a logic puzzle, like the ones we work on every day in our work. We take all the known factors and we put them together into an equation to determine the unknowns. Do you agree so far?"

Paul nodded reluctantly, his lips pursed in a thin, impatient line.

"Good. I'll start by telling you exactly when, how and why I left Easterwood, since no one has bothered to ask me that." She explained, with some embarrassment, about the rock video and the colorful magazines in the dentist's office and the bus token she'd found on the floor. She repeated the voice mail message she'd left for Paul, which did not agree with the one he'd received.

"We can draw two possible corollaries from this conflicting evidence," she continued, her confidence growing. "One, Camille is lying." She wrote this down in a "possibles" column. "Two, someone altered the message. Now, Paul, why don't you tell me exactly how you discovered that M23 was missing. Humor me," she added when she saw that he hesitated.

To his credit, he played along. "I discovered the theft the morning after you left...."

Gradually the story unfolded. Baylor observed the give-and-take between Camille and her former employer as they hashed out the events of the past few days. She made notes, adding items to her "possibles" column, striking out others.

As he watched, a sudden conviction struck Baylor with the force of a mule's kick. She was telling the truth. She was innocent. Never mind the facts; there was no way in hell that his sweet, sexy Camille could be guilty of stealing.

On the heels of that realization came another: Baylor hadn't lost his instinct. It had been there all along, pushing insistently at his stubborn consciousness, trying to tell him the true score. Fear and self-doubt had caused him to turn a deaf ear when he should have listened. He could have cheerfully kicked himself in the rear for being so stubborn.

"What about the backup disks?" Camille was asking Paul.

"I tried them, but they seem to contain nothing but gibberish."

"Gibberish?" She instantly became more alert. "What kind of gibberish?"

"Just lines and lines of what look like comic-book curse words," Paul answered.

"Let me see them," she demanded excitedly as she fished in her backpack and extracted a set of keys. She handed them to Nita. "Could you go to my apartment and get something for me?"

"Of course," the older woman answered, though she looked to Paul for a confirming nod.

"By my computer there's a plastic file full of diskettes," Camille continued. "Just bring the whole box to the computer room."

Baylor had to struggle to stop himself from blurting out his newfound faith in Camille. He wanted to tell her—tell everybody—that he believed in her, and that he would help her prove her innocence. But he held himself back. He shouldn't tip his hand too soon, he decided. If Camille wasn't the guilty party, then someone *had* framed her, and it might very well be Paul or Nita.

The two men and Camille filed down the hall to the glassed-in, climate-controlled room that housed the isolated mainframe computer. While they waited for Nita, Paul turned over the "gibberish" disks to Camille. She called up a file using the special program required to work on M23, then examined the meaningless strings of consonants, asterisks, dollar signs and other nonsensical characters.

"Well?" Paul asked impatiently.

She shrugged. "I can't tell anything . . . yet."

Nita returned a few minutes later, breathless as if she'd been walking very fast. "I'm sorry I took so long," she said, handing the box to Camille. "I had a little trouble with the lock." She backed toward the door and hovered there, as if she were afraid the huge computer would do her damage.

Camille opened the file box and extracted her word-processing program, then fit it into the disk drive. This time, when she called up one of the "gibberish" disks, familiar words and sentences appeared on the screen.

"My notes!" she cried triumphantly. "See there? This is my personal journal. Obviously someone switched labels between these and the M23 backup disks."

"Obviously," Paul said without much conviction.

Baylor leaned over Camille's shoulder and read what was on the screen. It appeared to be a description of a high school dance, and it sounded very much as though it were a passage from a shy teenager's diary. The brief account made him want to fold her into his arms and comfort the lonely, unhappy child she must have been.

"Oh! You're not supposed to *read* it, Baylor," she said, punching a button and obliterating the text. "But you can see that these are the notes I described to you the other day. You probably thought I made up that stuff about the book I'm going to write, didn't you."

"What book?" Paul asked sharply.

As she briefly explained to a skeptical Paul about the proposed survival manual for gifted children, Baylor rejoiced silently. Here, at last, was a piece of evidence supporting Camille's claim. Not that he needed convincing anymore, but Paul did.

"I understand what you mean," Paul was saying. "Yes, someone obviously switched disks and labels. But why couldn't that someone have been you?"

"I would never leave years' worth of my notes behind," Camille countered.

Paul seemed to digest this for a few moments. "I'm willing to keep an open mind. Let's go back to my office and look at the 'equation' some more. Maybe we *can* treat this thing like a logic problem."

As they all filed out of the small computer room, Baylor reached over to give Camille's hand a reassuring squeeze, a secret message that he was on her side. Instead of accepting the comfort, small though it was, she jerked her hand away and threw him a look that could have scorched butter.

Her scorn hurt, but he couldn't blame her for being angry. He thought back to the cold, unfeeling way he'd thrown around his accusations, as if *he* were the injured party. He recalled the hurt look on her face, and the stubborn set of her chin when he'd so graciously offered his "support" if only she'd confess. He'd acted like a close-minded horse's petoot. Paul, at least, had opened his mind to explore all the possibilities.

Now that Baylor was thinking more clearly, perhaps he could be of some use in discovering the real culprit, he thought. He might not have Camille's finely tuned deductive reasoning powers, but he'd always been damn good at reading people.

At least, he used to be.... *No, I am good,* he corrected himself, refusing to let that crippling self-doubt creep in again. He'd find the scumbag who had framed Camille or die trying. But he had his work cut out for him. The real thief had to be exceedingly clever to have woven such a convoluted web of misinformation around Camille.

As they all settled back into their chairs in Paul's office, Baylor surreptitiously studied his three companions. Camille seemed outwardly confident, inwardly terrified, as well she might. Her reputation was at stake, and the threat of an arrest still loomed ominously on the horizon as long as those physical components remained at large.

Baylor studied her intensely, until her image blurred and was replaced with a disturbing mental picture of her petite form huddled in a cold jail cell. He simply wouldn't allow that to happen, he vowed fervently. The repugnant notion spurred him to think harder.

He shifted his attention to Paul, the man who had been his best friend since college. Though their personalities

were strikingly different, the two men had always agreed
on important matters—honesty and integrity. It was Paul
who had encouraged Baylor to move from Texas to Boston and join the police force here.

Though it seemed unthinkable that Paul could be the
guilty party, Baylor now knew better than to dismiss any
possibility out-of-hand. He'd already made that mistake
once today, by refusing to listen to Camille. He forced
himself to study Paul, whose hands were shaking slightly.
Nerves? Guilt?

Baylor focused his attention on Paul's eyes, the part of
the anatomy which most often reflected truth or deception. The other man's gaze was firm and direct when he
spoke. He seldom blinked. He seemed genuinely interested in digging to the truth.

Satisfied, Baylor slid his gaze from Paul to Nita, who sat
unobtrusively to one side taking notes. She hadn't offered
a single word, as if she preferred to wait for everyone else
to unravel the facts. Her face was impassive. But one of her
feet, encased in an orthopedic shoe, tapped relentlessly
against the carpet.

Nita was nervous.

Baylor ruthlessly studied the woman. Her outward appearance was that of someone's grandmother. She would
have looked more at home in a kitchen baking cookies. But
there was something about her that didn't sit right. No one
thing, perhaps, but a lot of details that were...wrong
somehow.

She played the granny part too well—the stooped pos-
ture, the cap of silver pincurls, the ancient cardigan habit-
ually draped over her shoulders and secured with a sweater
guard, the cat's-eye glasses, the hearing aid, the support
hose—Nita wasn't an old woman, she was a caricature of

one. She was overflowing with "nice old lady" tags. Why had he never noticed before?

"It's possible—barely possible—that someone framed you," Paul was saying grudgingly to Camille. He stretched elaborately. "I don't know about the rest of you, but I could use some coffee."

"I'll get it," Nita said, quickly excusing herself.

A scenario began to gel in Baylor's mind. It was improbable, at best, and yet it would explain a lot. How could he test his theory?

When Nita returned a short time later, she carried not the tray with the silver coffee service, as Baylor had expected, but a single white envelope with Paul's name scrawled across it. The seal was broken. Appearing embarrassed, she handed it to Paul.

"The day after Camille left I found this on my desk, mixed in with some other papers," she said. "I should have given it to you a long time ago. But since you'd already determined that Camille had taken M23... Please understand—I just wanted to spare you the pain. Her words are so harsh..."

Baylor's eyes darted from Nita to Paul, who was scanning the computer printout he'd extracted from the envelope. His face turned almost gray as he read. Then Baylor looked at Camille, who watched anxiously, her brows drawn together in a perplexed expression.

"What is it?" she finally asked.

Without a word Paul tossed it across his desk, more toward Baylor than Camille. But it was Camille who stood to reach the paper, then slowly sank back into her chair as she read it. She closed her eyes and shook her head, then dropped the letter onto the desk as if it had suddenly burned her fingers.

Since no one seemed anxious to clue him in, Baylor picked up the letter and read it. It appeared to be a typed confession from Camille. "You'll be reading this after I'm gone," it began. Mostly it was a virulent attack—against her father, against Paul, and against Easterwood Energy Institute, all of which had stolen her youth, the letter claimed. She had taken Project M23 out of revenge.

The explanation fit in remarkably well with the reasons Camille had already given for her departure from Easterwood. Yet the wording simply didn't sound like Camille, and she'd looked too shocked as she'd read it. Baylor knew without question she'd never seen it before.

Paul reached for the phone. "I'm calling security."

"Wait a minute, I didn't write that," Camille objected, her voice high and sharp with near-panic.

"I'd like to believe you didn't," Paul said calmly, though he obviously still smarted from the letter's harsh words. "However, the letter was produced on your personal printer. There's not another printer in the whole complex with that distinctive typeface. Also I might point out that your computer automatically records the time and date of each document at the bottom as it prints. This one is dated on the afternoon before you left Easterwood. And since you yourself said you told no one of your plans to leave, I don't see how anyone but you could have written that confession."

Camille had picked up the paper and was studying it anew. When she put it down again, her face crumpled in despair. "I didn't do it—Paul, you have to believe me." And at Paul's hard expression, she turned first to Nita, then Baylor. "Doesn't anyone believe me?"

Baylor sneaked a peek at Nita. He caught just a brief flash of smug satisfaction in the older woman's face before her placid expression returned, but that was more than he needed to see.

"I believe you, Camille," he said in a loud, sure voice.

Chapter Nine

"Well it's about time!" Relief coursed through Camille's every vein. Before she could think of what to say or do next, she'd launched herself out of her chair and toward Baylor. If he hadn't reflexively stood up to catch her, she would have ended up in his lap. Her arms flew around his neck, and she hugged him long and hard.

After a stunned moment he returned her hug, his palms warm and reassuring against her back.

"Baylor, has your brain gone soft?" Paul shouted. Though she couldn't see him, Camille could just imagine his face. His eyebrows were undoubtedly arching so high they'd almost met up with his hairline.

"I think I've just now come to my senses," Baylor answered, giving Camille one last squeeze before firmly setting her away from him. But his blatantly trusting gaze continued to warm her from the inside out. She could feel her skin flushing until she knew she must be the color of a healthy salmon.

Only moments before she'd been sure the whole world had conspired to find her guilty of something she hadn't done. With just a few firmly spoken words, Baylor had changed her entire outlook. As long as he stood in her corner, she knew she could survive whatever else happened.

She opened her mouth to say something, but instead a sob escaped, an uncontrollable result of combined anxiety and relief, frustration and gratitude, as well as a host of feelings she couldn't even give name to. The sob multiplied into several, with a full accompaniment of copious tears and noisy sniffles.

"It's time to take a break," Baylor said decisively as he guided her to her chair. He touched the back of her neck, then started a slow, soothing massage. The tight muscles there melted like honey warmed by the sun, and she began to breathe almost normally.

"Oh, the coffee," Nita said with a nervous flutter, laying down her notebook. "I forgot all about it." She exited the room with her usual quiet efficiency.

Paul, too, looked anxious to be anywhere but where he was, obviously uncomfortable in the face of Camille's emotional outburst. As he stood he crushed out the cigarette that had been burning untended in the ashtray. "I suppose we could all use a few minutes to clear our heads—especially you, Baylor." He gave Baylor a meaningful glance before leaving.

Camille's crying bout stopped as suddenly as it had started. Embarrassed, she looked around the room for a box of tissues so she could mop her tear-streaked face, but she didn't see one. She knew she looked frightful, and though her appearance shouldn't have mattered just then, it did. She was about to bolt for the ladies' room, but

Baylor held her fast, his hands anchored firmly on her shoulders.

"Don't go."

At the note of urgency in his voice, she doubled her efforts to pull herself together, rubbing at the wetness on her face with the heel of her hand.

Baylor brushed at the lingering moisture with his own fingers, then gently kissed away an escaping tear. "First I want to tell you how sorry I am." He leaned his head against hers, so that his breath tickled her hair. "I shouldn't have ever doubted my instincts about you."

She reached up to touch his face, just to be sure he wasn't some figment of a hopeful imagination. "You believe me about everything now, don't you?"

"Everything," he assured her.

"I didn't know I had the M23 disks—"

"I believe you." He leaned down until his face was just inches from hers.

"And that package I mailed—I didn't know what was in it—"

"Yes, sweetheart, I know." He moved even closer.

"And that letter—"

"Of course you didn't write it."

"But how did you—"

He silenced her last doubt with a kiss, pressing his mouth against hers in a tender gesture, which rapidly increased in intensity. He pulled her out of the chair and molded her body to his, holding her so tightly she couldn't have broken free even if she'd wanted to. In the back of her mind she knew they shouldn't be doing this, not here and now when Paul or Nita could return at any moment. But somehow she couldn't summon the courage to put a stop to it.

"When this is over..." he murmured against her lips.

"Yes, I know," she whispered.

He cupped her face in his hands and searched her eyes with his. "You're not afraid, are you?"

"Not with you."

"I wouldn't hurt you. Never again." He brushed his lips against the fading bruise on her cheek, but she knew he was referring to other hurts, too, the kind that don't show on the surface. "I'm not too proud of the way I treated you earlier," he continued after a few moments. "I said some things . . ."

"Forget about it. That's over now."

"I can't forget about it."

"Then how about I let you make it up to me?" She gave him a patently seductive smile, wondering if she might be making a fool of herself. But if she was, she may as well do it right. Turning suddenly serious, she reached up to grasp both of his hands with hers. "Baylor, when you feel something way deep inside, and it kind of hurts but it feels good and it makes you want to laugh and cry at the same time—is that normal, or do I need psychoanalysis?"

He didn't laugh at her silly question, as she'd expected him to. "Sounds like you're coming down with something. Maybe you caught it from me." He kissed her again, with agonizing thoroughness, spearing her mouth with his tongue, in and out, in and out. She tilted her hips against his in an effort to bring them closer together and wished desperately that they were anywhere but in her former boss's office.

A groan escaped from somewhere deep in Baylor's throat. He slid his hands down her neck, along her collarbone and to her small, firm breasts. He'd never touched her there before. First he felt her tremble in response to the intimate caress, and then he became aware of his own reaction. Like flashes of lightning rippling across a night sky, their sinuous movements and sighs of arousal played off each other.

Camille had the power to tempt a saint, Baylor thought, and he was far from saintly. With some effort he lifted his mouth from hers. "Much as I'm enjoying myself, Smart Stuff," he said in a ragged voice, "we'll have to continue this another time. We still have some hot water to get you out of."

"Hmm? You want me to take a bath?" she asked dazedly.

He chuckled. "Hot water. It means trouble."

"Oh, that." With her head against Baylor's chest, she breathed deeply until she could think clearly again. "You mean it's not enough that you believe me. We still have to convince everyone else I'm innocent."

"And the way to do that is to expose the guilty party." Baylor pulled away and released her, turning suddenly businesslike. "I know who set you up. But I can't prove it yet. You've got to help me do that."

"Not Paul?" She scarcely breathed the question.

"No. Nita."

"But that's not poss—" She stopped herself. If Baylor thought Nita was guilty, then Camille believed him. "How? She's terrified of computers."

"Or she pretends to be. For all we know she could be a computer expert. Maybe she's been hiding a number of talents behind that old-lady facade, biding her time until M23 reached a stage that it would be worth the risk to steal it. She figures no one would suspect her for the very reason you stated. And she was almost right."

"Are you saying Nita's some kind of computer-whiz-corporate spy?" Camille asked. "But that's so..."

"Improbable?" He shrugged. "Maybe. I'm only guessing. But if you didn't write that letter..." He picked

up the odious piece of paper from the desk, where he'd
dropped it earlier, and waved it in the air for emphasis.
"... and you didn't tell anyone of your plans to leave
Easterwood, there remains one inescapable conclusion—"

"The letter was written after my departure." Camille
finished for him.

"Exactly. How about this time and date printed at the
bottom?" he asked. "Could it have been falsified?"

"Sure." She took the letter from Baylor and studied it
again, pacing restlessly, the confidence she'd felt earlier
returning. "Whoever did this went into the setup program on my computer and changed the time and date,
that's all. It takes just a minute or two."

"You know what I think?" Baylor said. "I think that
when Nita went to your apartment a few minutes ago to
fetch your disk file, she did just that. She reprogrammed
your setup, or whatever you said, and then dashed off that
letter. When she saw that Paul was beginning to listen to
you, she whipped out her manufactured evidence as a last,
desperate attempt to implicate you."

"It worked, too, didn't it," Camille said with a shiver.
She scrutinized the letter once again, then grew very still,
concentrating on the time and date. "Wait a minute. Oh,
wait a minute, Baylor. I *couldn't* have written this, not at
that time on that day. I was sitting in the dentist's chair at
exactly that moment!" She laughed giddily, her emotions
unnaturally heightened by all the preceding drama.

Baylor rubbed his hands together in triumph. "Now
we're getting somewhere. Someone definitely falsified that
time-and-date printout. Paul can't deny that."

Camille's smile faded. "He'll say *I* did the falsifying.
Just like he believes I switched the labels on those disks.

And we'll *never* convince him Nita is the guilty party. How do you know she did it, anyway?''

Baylor shrugged. "I could see it in her eyes."

"Instinct?" Camille queried, arching one eyebrow.

He nodded sheepishly. "Guess it came back."

"You never lost it to begin with," said Camille smugly. "I knew it all along. But we can discuss that later. Right now the question is, how could Nita have framed me when she didn't know I was leaving?"

"Are you sure she didn't know?"

"Positive. And I have another question. How was she planning to get the disks back?"

"I assume she made another copy of the data for herself. While all the hoopla about you was going on, she could have quietly disposed of her copy."

"But..." Camille thought for a moment. Something wasn't right about Baylor's supposition.

"What is it?" he asked.

"She couldn't have made a copy. M23's antitheft safeguard wouldn't have allowed her to make a clean copy of the data, from the hard disk or the backup diskettes. That," she said, pointing to the grimy white box still sitting on Paul's desk, "contains the only M23 data still intact. Which means..."

They looked at each other and exchanged a conspiratorial smile. Baylor voiced the thought that had occurred to both of them. "Nita didn't know you were leaving. She stashed the disks in your apartment, planning to retrieve them later. You must have put quite a kink in her plans when you disappeared with the only viable copy of M23."

The sound of the doorknob turning halted further speculation. The door opened a crack, then Paul stepped one foot into the room and stopped, half inside and half outside. He looked pale and unsure of himself—a far cry from the loud, blustering man who had departed a few minutes earlier.

Camille instinctively moved closer to Baylor, so that they presented a united front. "We have something to discuss with you, Paul," she said, taking control of the conversation while she had the nerve. "Privately," she added, "before Nita gets back. I didn't write that letter, and I've got some pretty convincing evidence in my favor."

"I know you didn't," Paul said in a shaky voice. He shrugged apologetically before stepping farther into the room, pushing the door open as he did to reveal Nita standing behind him. In her hand was a dark, deadly-looking gun pointed at the small of his back.

Camille reflexively gasped and clutched at Baylor's sweater. He put his arm around her shoulders and hugged her to him protectively. "We were going to try to convince you that Nita was your thief," he said to Paul. "Guess that's not necessary now."

Nita, minus her thick glasses, was standing straight and looking quite a bit younger and more robust than she had before. She nudged Paul across the room until he was standing with Baylor and Camille. "That's enough chit-chat," she said brusquely, eyeing each of them in turn. The gun's short, snubby barrel followed her gaze. After a few moments she singled out Baylor. "Mr. Pierce, would you be kind enough to hand me your gun?"

"Ever polite, eh, Nita?" he said. "Unfortunately I don't have a gun." He held his arms straight out to the sides. "Body search if you want."

"I'm not stupid enough to get that close to you," said Nita. "I never underestimate a cop. I knew you were on to me the moment you defended Camille. Take off your sweater."

"What?"

"You heard me."

Baylor complied with a shrug, peeling the cream-colored sweater over his head to reveal his white sleeveless undershirt. He tossed the sweater aside, then turned in a slow circle for Nita's benefit.

There was no way he could hide anything in those snug jeans, Camille caught herself musing quite inappropriately. She felt a catch in her throat as the realization hit her that she could die today, die without ever knowing the joy she and Baylor could have discovered together. She vowed silently to keep on the alert. If anyone could get them out of this jam, Baylor could, but he might need her help.

Nita seemed satisfied that Baylor carried no weapon. "I won't even bother with you two," she said, nodding toward Camille and Paul. "I can't imagine either of you carrying a gun, much less knowing how to use it."

Baylor's brain worked furiously, cataloguing Nita's traits as they appeared. She was no amateur. And she was ruthless. She knew her weapon and she wouldn't hesitate to use it, if that became necessary to carry out her scheme. On the other hand, she wasn't the sort to kill just for the sake of it. If they all cooperated with her, they would live. And to hell with M23. She could have it.

He also noted her self-satisfied smile. She knew she was clever, and she enjoyed lauding her superiority over them. *Get her talking,* he thought. She was the type who would savor bragging. If he could persuade her to talk about herself, maybe she'd get overconfident and make a mistake.

"So, Nita, what are your plans?" he asked conversationally.

"I should think that would be obvious to a seasoned detective like yourself, Mr. Pierce," she answered, looking down her nose at him as she picked up the white box and stuffed it into the pocket of her cardigan. "I'm going to deliver this data as promised. But first I'm going to lock the three of you in the laboratory, where you can amuse yourselves for a couple of days. It'll be at least Monday before anyone even misses you. By the time they figure out where you are and penetrate your security measures, I'll be long gone." She pushed the office door open wide, then stepped away from it. "Proceed ahead of me, please. You all know the way."

The tomb, Baylor had always called Paul's windowless lab. He didn't relish being locked in there without food for any length of time, but at least Nita intended to let them live. He took Camille's hand and gave it a reassuring squeeze before he guided her toward the door. This time she smiled bravely and squeezed back.

"I have just one question for you, Nita," Baylor said as he allowed Camille and Paul ahead of him. "How old are you really?"

"Forty-seven," she said with obvious pride. "Not that it's any of your business. Go on, follow them." She gestured with her gun.

"Just for future reference, I'd tone down your old-lady act if I were you. It's too obvious. That's part of what tipped me off."

"Yeah, well, it didn't tip you off soon enough, did it," she said smugly from several feet behind him. "I've had Paul fooled for five years. *Five years* I've been waiting to pull this off. And to think the mousy little genius almost ruined everything."

Camille's shoulders stiffened at the derogatory reference, and Baylor felt a pang of empathetic pain. *Oh yes,* he thought. Nita had quite an ego, and she fed it by put-

ting other people down. "Is your real name J. Cordaro?"
he asked her, taking a stab in the dark.

She laughed as the short, tense parade rounded a corner. "Juanita Cordaro is one of several very credible
aliases I've adopted over the years, complete with social
security numbers, credit histories, and drivers' licenses.
Guess I won't be using her for a while."

She seemed eager to talk. She hadn't even noticed that
his "one question" had multiplied. "How did you plan to
retrieve the data from Camille?"

Nita snorted. "I didn't. I had a copy of my own to sell.
It wasn't until my buyer checked out the diskettes that I
found out the copy I'd taken was flawed—had glitches all
through the data."

So, Camille was right about the antitheft device.

"But . . ." Nita continued breezily, "that doesn't matter
now. I have a clean copy, and soon I'll have my payment
and be on my way."

"But why did you bother to make Camille look guilty?"
Baylor persisted, more out of his own curiosity than anything. He wanted to understand all the details of Nita's in-
tricate plan, and since she was being obligingly chatty, he
figured it couldn't hurt to ask. "Why didn't you just copy
the data and sell it? Then no one would have discovered the
theft."

"You're forgetting the physical components. The project is no good without those, and they would have been
missed sooner or later. I made Camille my scapegoat so no
one would suspect me, of course. It would have worked,
too, if she hadn't run away. I'd planned to cast just enough
suspicion on her so Paul would search her apartment. He'd
have found the disks, Camille would have been fired—or
she might have gone to jail, who knows?—and no one

would have suspected sweet little Nita Carter. I'd have taken retirement in another couple of months."

"Oh, well," she concluded as they reached the locked entrance to the laboratory. She tossed a handful of keys to Paul, indicating he should open the double steel doors. "So my retirement comes a little earlier than I'd planned."

"Nita," said Paul, hesitating as he held the key poised over the lock. "I'm begging you, don't do this. Don't all the years we've spent working together mean anything?"

She gave a loud, derisive laugh. "Working together? Is that what you call it? 'Yes, Paul, I'll get those memos typed right away,'" she said, recalling her subservient "Nita voice" with ease. "'Would you like some coffee, Paul? Cream, no sugar, just the way you like it. Yes, of course I'll work late. No, I don't mind picking up your dry cleaning and paying your personal bills.' That's not working together. That's a master and his dutiful slave."

Paul appeared bewildered. "You never once indicated any displeasure in our working relationship."

Nita cackled again. "Let me tell you, it was tough sometimes not to tell you to go to hell, but the good-little-secretary act was all part of the scam. C'mon, unlock that door. I don't have all day."

As Paul's hand remained poised above the lock, Baylor studied the obvious war of emotions on his friend's face and dreaded what might come next. Paul had never been the heroic type, but desperation could change that.

He seemed to come to a decision. He straightened, facing Nita with a determined set to his jaw. "You could never shoot me, Nita," he said, sounding quite sure of himself. "We've been through too much together."

Nita's faded blue eyes snapped to attention, and the smugly superior expression fell away. Since she was the one holding the gun, clearly she hadn't expected any guff.

"Don't test me, Paul," she said, wiggling the gun for emphasis. "I don't even need a good excuse to shoot you. I could do it just thinking about all that coffee I served you, cream no sugar."

Paul chanced a sideways glance at Baylor. "She's bluffing," he said, as if apologizing for her.

"No, she's not," Baylor said emphatically, more sure of this than he had been of anything in his life. He found himself comparing this situation to that other hostage incident. The two were eerily similar. But unlike that cold, snowy night, in this instance Baylor was one hundred percent sure of what he saw and what he knew. Nita Carter, or whoever she was, was as desperate as any person he'd seen holding a gun. She was just a little crazy, and she was quite capable of pulling the trigger. There was no arguing with his instinct this time. Baylor tried not to think about the damage a .22 automatic could do at this range.

Paul returned his attention to the older woman. "You're bluffing, aren't you, Nita." He took half a step toward her. "You can't actually shoot me, can you?" he said in a coaxing voice. "Now you're only guilty of stealing something. Shoot me and you'll be in prison the rest of your life. You don't really want to kill anyone. Why don't you drop the gun?" He took another step.

Nita trembled, just slightly. "You move one inch closer and you'll find out just how wrong you are, Paul."

"Listen to her, Paul," Baylor said urgently, sensing his friend's intention. "Trust me on this one, buddy. She'll shoot you."

"Do what she says," Camille pleaded. "No computer disks are worth dying for."

Paul didn't appear to be listening. He took another step, a longer one this time, and held out his hand. He was only a couple of feet from Nita now. ''Give the gun to me,'' he commanded.

Nita's index finger twitched as she tightened it on the trigger. At that exact instant Paul lunged for her. Baylor yelled out a warning, too late. The two bodies collided and the gun exploded.

At first Baylor thought Paul had been hit. The momentum of Paul's lunge had landed both himself and Nita on the floor, and neither of them was moving. But as Baylor tried to take a step toward them, he realized he couldn't breathe. Then he looked down to see an enormous crimson stain spreading across his undershirt and seeping onto his jeans.

God Almighty, he thought as his knees buckled. *It doesn't even hurt. How in the hell did I get shot and not know it?* That was his last coherent thought before his world went blissfully black.

Chapter Ten

The next few seconds seemed to move in slow motion for Camille. Like a movie camera panning a scene, she first took in Baylor's inert form and the blood soaking his undershirt. Her throat constricted into an almost-scream, but she stopped herself before panic could set in. Baylor needed her, and she would be of no use to him in hysterics.

Next she looked at Paul and Nita, where they'd crashed to the ground. At first she thought they were both unconscious, too, until Nita, trapped under Paul's sprawling form, began to grope around for something. The gun. Quickly Camille retrieved the weapon from where it had fallen onto the carpet, just as Nita was squirming her way out from under Paul.

Somehow, though Camille had never dealt with a real emergency, she knew what had to be done in order to save Baylor's life. With a cold fury, she pointed the gun at Nita. "Get up. Now!"

"You gotta be kidding," Nita said, though she obeyed the command. "You don't have the slightest idea how to use that—even if you had the guts to."

"Just try me." Camille didn't have time to trade barbs. "Pick up those keys and unlock the door."

Nita looked as if she might object. But if a smart retort was on the tip of her tongue, she stifled it in the face of Camille's deadly determination and did as she was told.

"Now go inside the lab and shut the door behind you," Camille said in a voice she could hardly recognize as her own. Nita obeyed, but with a small hiss of protest.

When the older woman was safely confined, Camille looked around desperately for something with which to secure the door, because it could always be unlocked from the inside. How had Nita planned to secure it? she wondered. Her gaze settled on Paul's belt. That would have to do. Keeping the gun trained toward the door, positive that Nita's passivity was only temporary, she worked the buckle with one hand.

Paul began to groan. His eyes sprang open just as the belt came free of his pants. "Ohhhh . . . oh my head . . . Camille? What the heck are you doing?" Then his gaze fell on Baylor. "Oh, dear Lord, what happened?"

"Find a phone and call an ambulance," Camille ordered as she struggled frantically to secure the belt through the handles of the double steel doors. "And call the police." Her normally sedate voice rang up and down the corridor.

Her fierceness mobilized him. "Right, I'll call 911," he said, pulling himself off the floor with no small effort. He shook his head once, as if to clear it, then took off down the hall at a lope.

Satisfied that Nita was temporarily neutralized and that help was on the way, Camille was finally able to turn her attention to Baylor. Fighting tears, she dropped onto her knees beside him and laid her ear against his chest.

He was alive. His breathing was rapid, but his heart thumped with reassuringly regularity.

The wild bullet had struck him on the right side, close to the bottom of his rib cage, and there was blood everywhere. Camille gingerly lifted the red-stained undershirt away from the ghastly wound and tried to recall anything and everything she'd learned of physiology. Had any of his vital organs been damaged?

She should try to stop the bleeding. Apply pressure to the wound—she remembered that from an Easterwood first-aid course she'd taken.

Lacking anything handy with which to soak up the blood, she removed her cotton blouse without a second thought, rolled it into a ball and laid it against the wound, pressing down with the heel of her hand.

Baylor groaned in protest.

"Are you awake?" she asked anxiously. "Baylor, say something."

His eyelids fluttered, until he managed to keep them open for long enough to gaze curiously at her. "Hey, Smart Stuff." His greeting came out in a hoarse whisper. "What are you doing with your shirt off?"

Camille looked down at herself, clad only in jeans and a transparent bra, but she was too terrified to be embarrassed. "I'm trying to stop you from bleeding. Am I doing the right thing?"

"I dunno," he slurred. "Whatever you're doin', it hurts like hell. You know, you look great without your shirt."

"Thanks," she muttered, not knowing what else to say to such a thing.

He paused a long while before speaking again. "If I die—"

"You *aren't* going to die!" she interrupted sharply as her eyes again filled with tears. He couldn't die. It was inconceivable.

He smiled weakly. "Good. 'Cause I wouldn't want to die without making love to you."

"You just hold on to that thought," she said with a brave smile. "Think about getting better so we can make love."

"Promise?"

"Promise."

He closed his eyes and sighed, and she knew he was unconscious again. But the smile stayed on his lips.

The police and paramedics arrived in a noisy crowd, with Paul heading up the rear, and for a few moments chaos reigned. Paul directed the patrolmen to the laboratory doors, where two of them set to work unfastening the belt. A man in a white uniform pulled Camille out of the way so another man could examine Baylor.

"Are you hurt, ma'am?" the paramedic asked, repeating the question several times when she failed to respond. Someone handed her a blanket. It was only then that she realized she was standing around half-dressed in front of six strange men.

"I'm not hurt," she finally managed, wrapping the blanket around her shoulders and clutching it in front of her breasts. "But Baylor—is he going to be all right?"

No one answered her.

She started to shiver in delayed reaction. All that blood—how could a person possibly live after bleeding so much?

A subdued Nita was being cuffed and informed of her rights as the paramedics were placing Baylor on the stretcher with professional efficiency. One of them was talking into a hand radio, but Camille couldn't hear what was being said. All she could do was to look on helplessly.

"Can you tell us more about what happened here?" one of the police officers asked. He was young and had a kind face, so Camille responded by trying to explain the odd circumstances leading up to the shooting. But after a few sentences she realized she was making little or no sense. Her mind was on the gurney that was disappearing around the corner.

Her knees were trembling, threatening to collapse beneath her and dump her on the floor, in fact. She looked down at the carpet and saw the blood stain, and thought she might just lose her lunch.

Finally she held her hands up in front of her face to ward off any more questions. "This will have to wait," she said sharply. "Someone I love might be dying, and I have to go with him."

Paul rounded the corner just then. He was out of breath, no doubt from running up and down Easterwood's hallways and opening various security doors. Camille pushed past the uniforms and ran toward him. She allowed him to give her a much-needed hug.

"Camille, honey, what happened to your clothes?" Paul quickly removed his suit jacket and put it around her shoulders, replacing the inadequate blanket.

She shoved her arms through the sleeves and wrapped the lapels around her, relieved to be modestly covered again. "I used my shirt to mop up the blood—" At the memory she started to tremble and feel queasy again.

"Come on, let's go to the hospital," said Paul, putting a supportive arm around her. "He'll be all right, you'll see. Baylor's strong as a bull."

"Are *you* all right?" she asked, only now remembering that he'd been briefly unconscious. "Did you hit your head?"

He nodded. "I have the king of all headaches, but nothing worse."

"Still, maybe you should see a doctor when we get to the hospital."

He waved away her concern. "I want to tell you, Camille, you did a great job back there. By the time I came to, you had Nita locked in the lab. How did you do it?"

Camille shrugged. "I don't really remember. All I could think about was getting that woman out of the way so I could help Baylor."

The black, syrupy brew that came out of the hospital vending machine didn't deserve to be called coffee, Camille decided. She put in lots of sugar and powdered cream and drank it anyway. At least it warmed her a little. She'd been cold, inside as well as out, ever since they'd taken Baylor away on that stretcher.

As the police had completed their questions in the emergency waiting room, a kind volunteer had provided Camille with a Boston Celtics sweatshirt, a definite improvement over Paul's jacket, but she still shivered from time to time.

She jumped when a hand touched her shoulder. She turned around to find Paul, his face etched with concern. "I couldn't find out much," he said. "The woman at the desk said he was being prepped for surgery. We might have a long wait ahead of us. Do you want to go down to the cafeteria and get something to eat?"

The thought of food made her stomach turn over. "No. You go ahead, though."

Paul shook his head. "I'm not hungry either." They ambled back to the waiting room, where a television blared unattended. A young Asian woman was reading Dr. Seuss aloud to her two children. Her accent made Camille think of In-Ho, which in turn made her think of the M23 disks, and she suddenly realized she didn't have any idea where they were.

She touched Paul's arm. "What happened to M23?" she asked casually, so as not to alarm him.

He thought for a moment, looking perplexed. "I don't know. Last I saw the diskettes they were in Nita's pocket. I suppose the police have them. Frankly at this point I don't care." He squeezed his eyes tightly closed. "I was thinking about M23 when I tried to get Nita's gun. I was thinking of all the work we'd put in on that project, and how I couldn't bear to see it go down the drain. You and Baylor tried to tell me it wasn't that important, but I didn't listen. Dammit!" he said with sudden forcefulness, clenching his fists impotently. "Why didn't I listen?"

"Surely you're not blaming yourself for what happened!" She took his hand into both of hers. "It was an accident, pure and simple. You did what you thought was right at the time, and you were incredibly brave."

"It didn't work out quite like I thought it would," he said grimly. "I thought I would rush Nita and wrest the gun away from her, saving the day. Instead I hit my head against the wall, knocked myself out, and got my best friend shot in the bargain. Some hero." He shook his head. After a pause he asked, "Are you still angry at me about the other stuff?"

She arched an eyebrow at him. "You mean for thinking I was a thief and a liar?" She left him in suspense for a brief moment before she gave his hand another squeeze.

"All's forgiven," she said, and she meant it. "Nita laid a very clever trap. I can't blame you for falling into it."

"I still can't believe Nita Carter..." He left the thought unfinished. "I don't suppose you'd consider coming back to work at Easterwood, would you?"

She shook her head, her mind definitely made up on this point. "It's time for me to move on. I've got some living to catch up on."

"And with whom do you plan to do that living?" Paul asked, his eyes narrowed in a calculating squint.

Camille could feel the color creeping up her neck. "Is it that obvious?"

"I'd have to be blind not to see it. Anyway, I heard you tell that police officer you loved Baylor."

That flustered her even further. She'd forgotten what she'd said during a moment of stress. It was true, of course. She did love him. But she wasn't sure she wanted anyone else to know just yet. "I was overwrought," she finally said, not meeting Paul's gaze.

"Might I offer a brotherly word of advice?"

"I could probably use one. Go ahead."

"Well, I'm not quite sure how to put this, but I'll just plunge ahead. You're not very...experienced when it comes to men—"

"Why don't you just spit it out?" Camille said good-naturedly. "I'm a virgin, okay? Let's let the whole world know."

"Yes, well," Paul stumbled, "what I meant was, Baylor has been around the block a few times. He's—"

"I understand that."

"I'm sure he's quite fond of you, that he cares about you..."

"But?"

"Just don't start dreaming of white picket fences, okay?"

"Paul, what *are* you talking about? Why would Baylor make me think of a fence?"

"I mean, don't get your hopes up about marriage," Paul blurted out. "I can't put it any plainer than that."

She almost giggled like a giddy child at the picture of herself and Baylor dressed in wedding attire, but she turned suddenly sober when she realized what Paul was trying to tell her. What if she was attaching more seriousness to the relationship than Baylor? He'd said he wanted to make love to her, but that was all he'd admitted.

"I just don't want to see you get hurt," Paul said, putting an affectionate arm around her shoulders in an attempt to soften the dire warning.

"Baylor would never hurt me," she objected.

"Not on purpose, of course," Paul agreed quickly. "But sometimes it happens even with the best intentions."

She digested this for a few moments. "Getting hurt is part of living, isn't it?"

Paul shrugged. "I guess so."

"Then I'm willing to take the risk," she said, more to herself than Paul.

They waited for what seemed an eternity, until finally a youngish, dark-haired woman dressed in surgical scrubs approached them. She looked at them questioningly. "Are you waiting for Baylor Pierce?"

"Yes," they said together, shooting out of their chairs as if they were jack-in-the-boxes.

"I'm Dr. Petrovich," she said, offering her hand to both of them. "I performed the surgery on Mr. Pierce. The bullet struck no major organs, but it did break one of his ribs and there is a lot of tissue damage. He also lost quite a bit of blood."

"But he'll be all right, won't he?" Camille asked almost frantically.

The doctor nodded reassuringly. "His condition is fair, but his vital signs are stable. I have every reason to believe he'll recover fully. I just wanted you to be prepared. He'll be very weak."

"Can I see him?" Camille asked.

"He's still in recovery. We'll let you know when he's ready for visitors."

The doctor departed, leaving Camille feeling both elated that Baylor had survived the surgery and disappointed that she couldn't visit him yet. She needed to see for herself that he was going to pull through. "That sounded good, didn't it?" she asked Paul. "Fair condition—that's okay, isn't it?"

"Fair is almost good," he answered. "What did I tell you? Strong as a bull."

They settled in to wait longer, but almost immediately they were interrupted by a harried-looking nurse.

"Are you Camille?" she asked. At Camille's anxious nod she looked relieved. "Thank God. I have a patient in recovery who's been bellowing for you since the moment the anesthetic began to wear off. He's threatening to get up and walk out of here if I don't produce you, and I swear I think he could do it, never mind the fact that he has a hole in his side the size of Old Faithful."

Paul gave Camille an encouraging nod. Weak with relief, she followed the nurse. If Baylor had enough energy to be quarrelsome, he couldn't be in too bad a shape.

She wasn't prepared for the sight of him, however. He was pale, almost as pale as the sheets on which he lay. His dark hair made a stark contrast with the paper-white skin. There were tubes—one going into his hand, one inserted in his arm. A monitor next to the gurney kept track of his heartbeat. And he was still—so still.

"He's floating in and out," the nurse said in a loud stage whisper. "He's very groggy when he wakes up. He seems to think something happened to you. If you can keep him quiet, that would help."

By the time Camille found a folding chair so she could sit by the gurney, Baylor's eyes were open and following her movements with glazed interest.

"Baylor?" she said softly. "Are you with me?"

He reached for her. When their two hands met, his grip was surprisingly strong. "Is that you, Camille?" he said in a hoarse whisper. "My eyes don't seem to want to focus."

"Yes, of course it's me."

"You're not hurt?"

"Not in the least."

"I had this dream about you," he said in a thready voice. "You were running around without a shirt. And there was all this blood..." He swallowed noisily. "It wasn't a dream, was it?"

"No." She blinked back the tears that threatened. She needed to be strong just a while longer. "But you're the one who got hurt. Nita shot you. Remember?"

He nodded. "Sort of."

"The doctor says you'll be just fine."

"Damn right I'll be fine," he assured her in a deceptively strong voice. "I'm going to make love to you just as soon as—"

"Baylor, shh!" Camille was sure his words carried to every corner of the recovery room. A titter of laughter from the other side of the curtained partition confirmed her suspicion.

"You promised," he said, oblivious to the fact that he'd announced his amorous intentions to the world at large. "I remember."

"Yes, I promised," she soothed, putting her hand against his cool, dry forehead.

He closed his eyes and smiled, wearing the look of a child who's been promised a pleasant dream if he'll take a nap. She held his hand and watched him doze, loving him so much it hurt. She kept her index finger on his wrist, taking reassurance from the pulse she felt there. She watched him breathe, watched the life-giving blood and glucose drip into his veins.

He was going to live, she assured herself.

When next he opened his eyes a few minutes later, he seemed much more lucid, barraging her with questions. "Is Paul okay?"

"He got a little bump on the head, that's all," she reassured him.

"Is M23 safe?"

She shrugged. "Paul's best guess is that the police have the diskettes. It's not really important now. Funny how a little bullet can change your priorities."

"And Nita? What happened after I fell?"

"I locked her in the lab." Camille preened a bit. "You should have seen me, Baylor. I picked up that gun and ordered her around like I knew what I was doing. Then I yelled at Paul to call an ambulance. It was like another personality took over my body. I was a regular Jambo," she said proudly.

"Jambo?"

"The tough guy in the movie. You know."

"That's *Rambo*." He laughed, then stopped abruptly as a pained expression crossed his face. "Ouch. Don't say anything else funny, okay, Smart Stuff?"

"I should be calling *you* 'Smart Stuff,'" she said. "You're the one who figured out Nita was the thief. You and your instinct."

"Hey, that's right. I figured out a puzzle that had you stumped. Does that mean I'm a genius?"

"You *are* a genius," she replied. And when he rolled his eyes, she hastened to explain. "This thing you call 'instinct' is nothing more than a right-brain form of genius. It's not some magic gift from the gods," she added when he looked at her doubtfully. "When you look at someone, and you somehow know whether they're lying or not, you're actually making an informed decision based on all sorts of subtle cues that your subconscious picks up."

"Come again?"

"Oh, never mind," she said, deciding he was still too woozy to grasp any complicated explanations. "But you never lost your instinct. Your self-confidence took a blow, that's all."

"And I'm a genius, huh?"

"Well don't get *too* smug about it," she teased.

He gave her another sleepy smile. "If you're right, that means we should have some real smart kids. Your logic, my instinct . . ."

Camille's heart jumped into her throat. What had he just said? But his eyes had closed again.

Maybe she'd imagined it. No, Baylor Pierce had just mentioned kids. Children. *Their* children.

When the nurse stopped by to check Baylor's condition, Camille couldn't resist asking her something. "Is he in his right mind?"

The nurse, a sixtyish, gray-haired cherub, laughed as she checked his IV tubes. "What's he doing now, threatening to run a marathon? Patients sometimes say pretty crazy things when they're recovering from anesthesia. Last month a young, good-looking appendectomy patient offered to fly away with me to Rio. His wife was holding his hand at the time. She had no sense of humor.''

Camille nodded. That must be it. Baylor had been delirious. She tried to hold on to that sensible thought, but the notion of having babies with him made her feel like singing. She might have, too, if she'd known the words to any songs.

Baylor opened his eyes to a dim room. Yuk, a hospital. Oh, yes, he remembered now.

He hurt. Funny, when that bullet ripped him open, he hadn't felt a thing. He wouldn't have even known he'd been hit if he hadn't seen the blood. Now it felt as if some internal organ was on fire.

It took him a moment to realize he wasn't alone. There was an angel hovering over his bed. Not the angel of death—she was too pretty for that. Must be an angel of mercy. ''Camille?''

''It's about time you woke up,'' she said impatiently. ''The doctor said your anesthetic wore off hours ago. You've been plain old asleep.'' Her broad smile belied the cross words. ''How do you feel?''

He considered lying. ''About as you'd expect,'' he hedged. His memory was coming into sharp focus now. As she poured him a cup of water, he recalled everything about the shooting. He remembered a few brief moments of lucidity before the ambulance arrived, when he'd seen Camille soaking up his blood with the shirt right off her back. She was some kind of lady. Even when he'd been afraid he was dying, he'd thought of making love with her.

Then he'd gotten mixed up, believing *she'd* been hurt. He remembered waking up in recovery holding her hand, and his elation over seeing her whole and healthy had nearly overwhelmed him. He'd been so relieved, in fact, that he'd babbled on about all kinds of silly things, including the subject of children.

Atta way to be subtle, he congratulated himself with a swift mental kick in the buns. It might have been smarter on his part if he'd thought to mention marriage before offspring.

How had she reacted to his overly frank talk? He couldn't remember.

He took a few slow sips of water. "So how bad off am I?" he asked, looking around at the various tubes and needles attached to him.

"They could have fixed it with a styptic pencil," she said, ruffling his hair. But then she frowned. "You're in good shape, really. But earlier we didn't know how bad it was. Paul called your parents."

Baylor made a face. "Did he have to do that?"

She shrugged. "They're on their way to Boston. Don't you want to see them?"

"They'll fuss, is all. This accident will give them plenty of ammunition. They'll try to talk me out of staying on the police force. Mother will ask me—no, she'll *demand* that I come back to Waco so she can nurse me to health. She'll offer me a 'nice safe job' in her office. Just wait and see."

"And what will you tell her?" Camille asked.

"I'll tell her I'm a cop, and I'll always be a cop," he answered without hesitation.

Camille beamed at him. "No more leave of absence?"

He shook his head. "I'm back to work as soon as they'll let me. Hey, you want to do me a favor?"

"Anything."

"When my mother starts threatening to fly me back to Texas on a stretcher, kindly inform her that you've already got dibs on being my private nurse."

"Gee, I don't know, Baylor. I mean, I'll be happy to take care of you, but I don't want to antagonize your parents."

"Don't worry. The folks will be crazy about you no matter what you do. They'll probably like you better than they do me."

"Baylor! What a thing to say!"

"Well, you are an exceptionally accomplished woman. You're one of *them*."

"I am not," she said hotly, as if he'd insulted her. And maybe he had. "They might have liked Camille the Nuclear Physicist, but how will they feel about Camille the jobless writer?"

Baylor laughed, then immediately wished he hadn't. "Don't worry," he said again. "They'll be real anxious to make you one of the family." At her startled expression he realized he'd again blurted out something prematurely, and he didn't have the excuse of anesthesia this time. "Seriously, Camille," he began, but suddenly he found the words perversely difficult.

"It's okay," she said, looking anywhere but at him. "I'm sure that wasn't what you meant to say."

"No, it wasn't," he agreed. "What I meant to say was that *I'm* anxious to make you one of the family."

She stared at him, her big hazel eyes even bigger than usual.

"Maybe I'm a little too anxious," he added. "We've known each other less than a week. But dammit, I've seen all I need to see. I love you and I want to marry you." There, he'd said it. "Not immediately, of course," he added when she didn't jump at his proposal.

"Of course," she agreed, raising one eyebrow quizzically.

"I mean, you've only been away from that tomb at Easterwood for a few days. You have so much living ahead of you. You should travel...climb a mountain, or go on safari. I don't have the right to tie you down right now. But maybe in a year or two..."

She pursed her lips, then asked, "Does this have anything to do with white picket fences?"

"Sure, we could buy a house with a fence," he answered carefully, not quite sure where her peculiar question might lead.

"Baylor, I—" She halted, taking a tissue from the box by his bed and dabbing the corners of her eyes. "It seems I've done my share of crying today."

"Are you happy or sad?"

"Happy," she answered without hesitation. "How else should I be when my every wish is about to be granted?"

"Tell me what you're wishing for," he urged.

Her answer surprised him. "A lot of new clothes. A cozy little apartment in Charlestown—something like yours, maybe with bigger closets. A new computer—with a sixty-meg hard disk—so I can write my book. And, oh yes—" She fluttered her eyelashes at him.

He could have sworn she was flirting.

"Children. Lots of smart babies. Or maybe they won't be so smart. That's okay, too."

"And did you wish for a husband to go with the babies?"

"I guess that would make sense, wouldn't it."

"Stop teasing," he admonished. "I want a straight answer. Will you marry me? I'd get down on my knees if that were physically possible."

She gave him a mischievous grin. "Well, I do want a husband—preferably a smart police detective, one I'm desperately in love with. Do you meet those qualifications?"

He answered her by reaching up and grasping the end of her ponytail, then slowly pulling her toward him, offering her a predatory grin.

"Baylor, I'm afraid I'll hurt you," she protested, trying to maintain her balance so she wouldn't fall against him. When he kept on pulling, she had no choice but to succumb to his wishes, bracing her arms against the mattress on either side of his shoulders and leaning close.

She needn't have worried about hurting him. The moment her lips touched his, he felt no more pain.

*   *   *   *   *

Silhouette Romance ®

DIAMOND JUBILEE CELEBRATION!

It's the Silhouette Books tenth anniversary, and what better way to celebrate than to toast *you*, our readers, for making it all possible. Each month in 1990 we presented you with a DIAMOND JUBILEE Silhouette Romance written by an all-time favorite author! Saying thanks has never been so romantic....

If you missed any of the DIAMOND JUBILEE Silhouette Romances, order them by sending your name, address, zip or postal code, along with a check or money order for $2.25 for each book ordered, plus 75¢ for postage and handling, payable to Silhouette Reader Service to:

In the U.S.
3010 Walden Ave.,
P.O. Box 1396
Buffalo, NY 14269-1396

In Canada
P.O. Box 609
Fort Erie, Ontario
L2A 5X3

Please specify book title(s) with your order.

January:	ETHAN by Diana Palmer (#694)
February:	THE AMBASSADOR'S DAUGHTER by Brittany Young (#700)
March:	NEVER ON SUNDAE by Rita Rainville (#706)
April:	HARVEY'S MISSING by Peggy Webb (#712)
May:	SECOND TIME LUCKY by Victoria Glenn (#718)
June:	CIMARRON KNIGHT by Pepper Adams (#724)
July:	BORROWED BABY by Marie Ferrarella (#730)
August:	VIRGIN TERRITORY by Suzanne Carey (#736)
September:	MARRIED?! by Annette Broadrick (#742)
	THE HOMING INSTINCT by Dixie Browning (#747)
October:	GENTLE AS A LAMB by Stella Bagwell (#748)
November:	SONG OF THE LORELEI by Lucy Gordon (#754)
December:	ONLY THE NANNY KNOWS FOR SURE by Phyllis Halldorson (#760)

Hurry! Quantities are limited.

SRJUB-1AAA

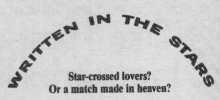

WRITTEN IN THE STARS

**Star-crossed lovers?
Or a match made in heaven?**

Why are some heroes strong and silent . . . and others charming and cheerful? The answer is WRITTEN IN THE STARS! Coming each month in 1991, Silhouette Romance presents you with a special love story written by one of your favorite authors—highlighting the hero's astrological sign! From January's sensible Capricorn to December's disarming Sagittarius, you'll meet a dozen dazzling heroes.

Sexy, serious Justin Starbuck wasn't about to be tempted by his aunt's lovely hired companion, but Philadelphia Jones thought his love life needed her helping hand! What happens when this cool, conservative Capricorn meets his match in a sweet, spirited blonde like Philadelphia?

The answer leads to THE UNDOING OF JUSTIN STARBUCK by Marie Ferrarella, available in January at your favorite retail outlet, or order your copy by sending your name, address, zip or postal code, along with a check or money order for $2.25 (please do not send cash), plus 75¢ postage and handling, payable to Silhouette Reader Service to:

In the U.S.
3010 Walden Ave.
P.O. Box 1396
Buffalo, NY 14269-1396

In Canada
P.O. Box 609
Fort Erie, Ontario
L2A 5X3

Please specify book title with your order. Canadian residents add applicable federal and provincial taxes.

JANSTAR